~ SUCKING DEAD ~

BOOK 3

SUCKING
HELL

ANDIE M. LONG

To everyone who wishes Gnarly Fell was real.
Maybe it's out there somewhere...
Andie xo

CHAPTER ONE

Dela

Callie and Lawrie's Wedding Day, Las Vegas

I stood in a chapel in Vegas and watched my sister, Callie, get married. As 'Elvis' declared them husband and wife, I saw my sister's new husband, Lawrie, look at Callie's best friend, Mya, and suddenly the newlyweds weren't there anymore. Lawrie had vampire whizzed them off somewhere.

"What's going on?" I barked out. There'd been enough shocks and surprises over the last few days seeing as someone had been trying to murder my sister. I'd thought we were past that now. Mya walked over to me while Bernard and Aria approached Elvis.

"He's just taken her to the Amazonian Rain-forest as she told me one of her greatest wishes was to be kissed in the rain," Mya explained.

"Oh, yeah, sure. I mean it's raining here in Vegas." I pointed outside of the chapel windows. "But of course let's just pop to the rainforest and give Callie's sister another heart attack. Do you know how much I will have aged this past week with all this stress?"

Mya tilted her head at me. "You're a fae. You live for hundreds of years. Now don't be so unromantic. Callie and Lawrie are having a movie-star moment alone as newlyweds. They'll be back before you know it."

I looked over Mya's shoulder and watched as Aria spoke to Elvis, his face taking on a glazed-over look. "So what's she telling Elvis? Not to be *Crying in the Chapel?* Asking him if he has a *Hound Dog* or any *Blue Suede Shoes?*"

Mya ignored my sarcasm. "She's telling him there's nothing untoward going on here and that the bride and groom are still present."

I watched as Elvis froze in place.

"So he'll come back to life when they re-appear?"

"Yes, and as we were the last wedding on his list, no one else will be kept waiting, so all is well."

"That's okay then. You carry on just fucking with people's heads so you can enjoy yourself. Bloody vampires."

Mya's eyes narrowed at me. "What's bitten your arse? You'd think you'd be ecstatic that you're at your sister's wedding instead of her funeral."

I exhaled. "I am. It's just... I hate weddings."

"They're not my bag either, Dela, but I'm not being a bitch about it all," she said in a low voice.

"I'm sorry." I sighed. "It's just they remind me I'm single. Very, *very* single."

"Ah, you poor thing. I just don't suit the colour white. I'm too pale now I'm a vampire. Plus, quickies might be okay for Callie, but I'd rather take my time. I've only been dating Death for two months. We still have a *lot* to learn about one another."

I realised the man himself was hovering at the back of Mya. I moved my head to see him better. "Hey, Death, is Elvis really dead, or was it all a conspiracy theory?"

"Wouldn't you like to know?" Death raised a brow.

"He'll not tell you. I've already tried all that and I can use blow jobs as persuasion, so you've no chance." Mya huffed.

At that point thankfully the bride and groom

returned and everything went back to normal. Well, as normal as it can get when you're at a wedding with vampires, fae, and Death himself. As they signed the register, I nudged Death who was now sitting next to me on a pew. "Look. I'm on Death row."

"Oh hahahahaha," Death replied, following it up with a smile.

I almost shit my pants. It was just... terrifying. Like a snake loosening its jaws before it swallowed you whole. The guy needed more practice at looking happy, otherwise we'd really be able to say he had a 'killer smile'.

"Aww, look at my boyfriend enjoying himself." Mya stroked his arm as she slid in at the other side of him. She stared up at him lovingly. "Shall we get out of here now, baby?"

"Yes, we'd better go see what the wayward are up to. I don't like leaving Spence keeping an eye on things. Since his romance with Jenny, he's continually distracted."

"Are you ready to say goodbye to your sister and for me to take you home?" Mya asked me.

"You go. I'll take her," said a voice from the back of me. I turned to see Lawrie's 'sister' Ginny in the pew behind. She was his sister in that they'd both been sired by the same Letwine vampire.

"Is that okay with you?" Mya checked.

"Yeah. It's fine. I might even hang around in Vegas for a while and get a flight home like normal people."

"You'd think having wings you'd be able to fly, wouldn't you?" Ginny commented. "I mean, I don't have wings, but I can zoom around, and you do have them and the most you can do is hover around in gardens and woodland. What a waste. It's probably because they're so flimsy." She felt at my wings, which I snapped back in. It made me ticklish when someone touched them.

The vampire attitude of superiority was really starting to grate on me. But not as much as all the soppiness appearing around me. Aria and Bernard were now smooching. My sister and Lawrie were liplocked, and Mya and Death were whispering sweet nothings to each other.

"Why do you think I'm offering to take you back?" Ginny whispered in my ear. "We're single and we're in Vegas. Let these lovesick fools go home and then we can party."

Suddenly things didn't seem so bad.

I hugged my sister. Truth was, I still had such mixed emotions. I'd been working through the agony of her potential demise and then suddenly that threat was gone, and she was getting married. Her and Lawrie had been in this love/hate relationship for so long that the fact they were now married would take some getting used to. But there was no doubt they were madly in love, and I was so happy for her.

I could only admit the bitter truth of my inner feelings to myself. She'd done it again. Got there first. I was a year younger and always playing catch up with Callie. I'd been dating like crazy to try and meet 'the one' and to get married first. I'd had a lot of fun, but I'd not met anyone who was marriage material, and now it didn't matter. Because I was the bridesmaid and she was the bride. And while I couldn't begrudge my sister anything due to the fact she was one of the kindest people who ever lived and I was so very thankful she was getting to carry on doing so, I felt a little lost.

"Earth calling Dela," Callie sing-songed.

"Sorry," I replied, coming back to my surroundings.

Callie and Lawrie had decided to take a week to honeymoon, given he could take them wherever they wanted to go. They'd be back for Christmas, although I no longer knew what the holiday season would be like for me anymore. It had always just been Callie and I, and now it wasn't. I needed a life of my own. It was time to make some changes, that was for sure.

"So, I closed the café for the week. Mya said she would keep an eye on the place, but if you would too, I'd appreciate it, seeing as Mya could be kept occupied by the wayward. I don't know what your plans are about whether you want to stay in the apartment over the shop now..."

"No. That's your place. I'm... buying my own house," I announced, which was as much news to me as the words left my mouth as it was to my sister.

"You are? Wow, that's amazing."

She was about to ask me more, but Lawrie appeared at our side. "Sorry to interrupt, but they need us out of here. Are you ready to go?"

I nodded at him, turning back to my sister. "I'll tell you all about it when you get back." *When I might know more about it myself.*

Everyone said their goodbyes and soon it was just Ginny and I left, standing outside the chapel.

"I'm pleased for my brother, but thank God that tedium is over," Ginny announced. "Vomit-inducing, the romance in that room."

"You don't want that for yourself?" I queried.

"God no. I just want a rich husband so I can live the most luxurious lifestyle without having to raise a finger. Why? Do *you* want that?"

"I thought I did," I answered honestly. "Now I'm not sure."

"Sister—and I'm going to call you that, cos now you kind of are—we are in Vegas. Let's go party. Forget about love and marriage; think money and winning lots of it."

I grinned at her. "Okay, let's go party."

We drank. We gambled. We drank some more. And we won, big time. Ginny was attracting those chips like she was guac. And then the next thing I knew, four big, burly security guys descended on us, two either side and we were 'accompanied' to a private room upstairs in the casino, where a guy who looked clean out of *The Godfather* sat in a black leather chair in front of an ornate desk. He watched us like a serial killer, assessing his prey as to locate the best place to slice first.

I trembled. What the fuck were we doing here? Did they not like people winning? Did they 'off them' quietly and then get back to business as usual, no one else the wiser that winners ended up in the Nevada desert? *Why can't I fucking fly properly?* I begged inside. I tried to hover but came up against resistance. *A ward. Interesting.*

"Good evening, ladies," Mr Mobster said, picking up his glass of scotch and taking a drink. I found that a bit cliché to be honest and wondered if a horse's head was about to be brought into the room.

"H-hi," I replied. 'You have a fine establishment, Mr...?"

"Russo. Armand Russo. And you are?"

"Dela Francis from Gnarly Fell in England. Actually, I need to get back as I'm looking after my sister's café while she's on honeymoon."

"Dela Francis. Fae if your freckles inform me correctly."

Damn fucking freckles. They landed in a pattern across my face that gave the game away to those in the know. Clearly, my twenty-four-hour lasting foundation was a big, fat liar.

"And now to your friend."

Ginny looked bored. "Virginia Letwine."

"Vampire," Armand said. "An uninformed vampire, working their mojo on unsuspecting patrons to get them to give you their chips in order that you could try to procure hearty winnings from my casino."

"You vampire-brainwashed people?" I admonished Ginny.

She just shrugged. "I'm a vampire, and my beauty alone wasn't getting them to part with their money. It was as if they were in the *thrall* of gambling in the casino."

Armand grinned and displayed fangs. Great, a mobster *and* a vampire. He'd no doubt torture me slowly, like shoot me in the knees and then drink from my wounds.

"So, you're one of the Russo clan? I thought they were based in Los Angeles?" Ginny queried.

"They are. However, I don't play well with others, so I came out here and set up my own little kingdom."

Ginny moved nearer and wriggled so her top fell down a little.

"As tempting as you look, sweetie, you come with a large side of desperation, and that is not attractive," Armand dismissed Ginny, who sighed heavily.

"So what's my punishment for trying to rip you off?" she asked.

"Nothing. You are a distant cousin of sorts. I just thought I'd bring you here so I could say hello and remove all of the chips you didn't actually win, which of course is all of them. I hope you enjoyed your evening though."

We gave up our chips and then said our good-byes. Security escorted us out of the building.

"Can we go back? I've actually had enough of being here," I asked Ginny.

"Sure. No doubt Armand has let all his business partners know we're around anyway, so we're not going to get rich here. I'll drop you back off at Gnarly and then go sulk in my room."

Placing her arms around me she whizzed me back to the fell.

It was around seven am and I staggered, holding onto the back of a bench in the boulevard, while I recovered my equilibrium.

"I'll stay until you feel all right," Ginny said.

It took me a few minutes and then everything came into focus, along with the noise. I stood up straight, facing in the direction of the cupcake café where a large crane stood. My mouth gaped open as

I took in the wreckage of the café. What the fuck was happening?

Recognising Nick Anderson behind the wheel of the crane, I began stomping in the direction of his vehicle. Ginny held me back just as he swung the wrecking ball straight through my apartment window.

What the hell?!!!

CHAPTER TWO

Nick

Gnarly's lift-cursing and engagement celebration. The day before Callie and Lawrie's wedding.

The feelgood factor in Gnarly was at an all-time high. Callie and Lawrie's falling in love and their engagement proved that the curse of Gnarly was indeed lifted and gave us all hope. You could see it in the expressions of every one of the villagers as we got together in the centre of the boulevard to celebrate. The place was trimmed up with pretty lights, but it was our eyes that twinkled the most. The atmosphere buzzed; giddy conversations and titters of laughter merged along with the background music playing on the speakers.

"Hey, Stan." Fenella's son Jason slapped me on

the back. Jason was my best mate and a dragon shifter and let's just say he could definitely be a bit... fiery.

"How many more times? I've changed my name."

"Fucking hell, St- Nick. I've known you for your whole thirty years since we were babes in arms. I can't just be expected to remember that every time. The residents of Gnarly will take ages to get used to calling you that, so just bloody get used to it."

"Hey, Nick. Jason." Milly and Tilly walked past and greeted us in stereo.

"They didn't have a problem remembering," I said snarkily, but Jason was too busy watching the twins as they walked down the boulevard to find somewhere to sit.

"Do you reckon they do *everything* together?" he said, hunger in his eyes.

"Please. Stop before I puke. Let's go find some-where to sit ourselves."

"Sure thing. I'm on it," he said, and I sighed as he hurried to follow Milly and Tilly.

Of course, he sat us directly opposite them, but then he ignored them, meaning I had to keep us engaged in polite conversation.

"What the fuck are you doing, Jase?" I whisper-hissed as the twins chatted with someone else for a time.

"Treating them mean, so they hunker after me, of course."

I gave up, left him to carry on with whatever daft mission he was on, and I turned and appraised the crowds until my eyes settled on a pretty, strawberry-blonde haired fae woman.

Delphinium Lily Alyssum Francis. Or Dela as she was known to all. She was dressed in a pale-green jumpsuit. The material looked silk-like, and when the soft breeze blew, the material flattened against the curves of her body. I wished I was nearer so I could see her face up close. She did her best to cover the fae freckles that scattered over her nose and cheeks, but they almost always fought through. I wanted to kiss each individual one.

"You're staring at her again, like some deranged stalker," Jase interrupted my reverie and pulled me back into the present moment.

"Thanks, buddy. Could have embarrassed myself there."

"I don't know why you don't just ask her out and have done with it," he said. "This crush has been going on way too long, and now you don't have the curse as an excuse anymore."

"Yeah, maybe," I mumbled in response, because I didn't want to tell him the truth. That I'd already asked her out two days ago and she'd told me she was too busy with Christmas.

It had taken me ages to get up the confidence to approach her at the counter of her sister Callie's cupcake shop where she worked occasionally, and not ask for yet another drink or sweet treat. I mean a diabetic coma was imminent that day and I didn't even have diabetes. It was just every time I'd gone to the counter, I'd chickened out. Finally, having got up the nerve to ask the question I'd practised in my head for years, I'd been met with her excuses.

My suggestion about after Christmas had been met with a change of subject. To make matters worse she thought my father being Father Christmas was a joke.

I needed a Christmas miracle. The irony that I was Santa's son was not lost on me.

The party was amazing and Fenella did a great speech about hoping we could all find our happy ever afters. I couldn't help but look over at Dela, and if she'd have looked back, I'd have felt there was a chance. But she didn't. Her focus was on her sister.

Of course it's on her sister. It's her sister's special day, you idiot.

My mind was always full of such excuses because I didn't want to face the truth. That Dela just wasn't into me.

Yet she was into a lot of others. It wasn't that she didn't date.

Dela was a known party-girl, always going out into London and enjoying date after date, though none of her suitors ever seemed to manage a second. My dad said she was clearly searching for something and not finding it, but whether that was her one true love or the biggest dick I didn't know. She was clearly finding the biggest dicks out there, just not located in their pants.

We all jumped as loud explosions sounded out in the near distance. "Someone's set the fireworks off by the sounds of it," Jason said. He'd helped set them up earlier. "I'd best go see what's happening."

"I'll come with you," I replied.

There was no point in me hanging around.

The fireworks had all been set off at once, creating a haphazard display in the sky. There was no one left around, so no clue as to who had done it and why. We secured the area with warning tape, put signs up saying to keep away for twenty-four hours, and said to Jase's mum that we'd be back tomorrow to clear it all up.

"What a shame we didn't get to enjoy them properly, just because some idiot decided to spoil the party," Fenella said.

"It's been amazing anyway," I told her. "You always been fantastic at throwing a good bash."

"Now the curse has lifted I'm hoping my son here will meet the love of his life and give me some grandbabies." She smiled at Jase who looked horrified.

"Steady on there, mother. The curse has only been lifted a month. Anyway, now you can go get yourself a big hunk of burning love."

"Your father was enough of one of those. Burned my house down. I happen to love where I live and prefer it standing."

Jase cut me a look. He'd heard this story many times as had I. These days they had medicines, spells, and potions to stop such accidents, but back then temper came at a price. Jase's dad had huffed and puffed and burned the house down.

"Anyway, we'd better get back to the boulevard and get on operation tidy-up," she said.

Jase groaned. "Why do you always organise all these events and rope me in?" He turned to me. "She'll have something else organised by tonight."

"I also have to help my parent tonight, so I can't stay too long to help you tidy up unfortunately," I informed Fenella.

"That's okay, Nick. We're all well aware of how busy a time of year it is for you," she replied. "You get on your way."

"No, I'll come help at the boulevard first," I insisted. It wasn't because I was interested in tidying up. It was to catch another glimpse of Dela. But when I got back, her, Callie, and the rest of their friends had gone.

I walked around the rear of Stan A's Hardware store. Most of the shop buildings had flats above the premises, but ours was a house, the front downstairs of which housed the shop. Around the back we had a large workshop in an L-shape that meant that in the centre was a rectangular shaped courtyard where we'd made wooden benches and a firepit. Dad and I quite often enjoyed a beer out here at the end of the day when neither of us had other plans.

I headed inside, cracked open a cold beer from the fridge and came to sit outside. Half an hour or so later my dad emerged from the workshop, wiping sweat off his forehead with his sleeve.

"Grab us one, will you, son?" he asked, dropping down onto another bench.

I did so, bringing it out to him, along with a damp cloth. He wiped his brow and face with the cloth, the friction making his cheeks go even ruddier than usual.

"How'd the celebrations go?" he asked.

"Great until someone set off all the fireworks as a prank."

"Oh dear. Fen won't have been happy."

"Nope. But like Jase said, she'll have another celebration planned by tomorrow. She's obsessed."

"It's how she dealt with her own heartbreak, son," Dad said, taking a mouthful of beer. "She threw herself into organising. First the rebuild of her house, and then she began with things for Gnarly. And it's meant a lot to us, because there was always someone falling victim to the curse and Fenella would bring them on board and distract them from their heart-break by keeping them busy."

"Fuck, I never realised."

"Language!"

"Sorry, Dad, but just whoa. This curse really messed everyone up, right?"

He nodded, staring toward the fire pit, and I knew he must be thinking about my mother. I intended to ask him one day soon about whether he'd thought of trying to track her down now the curse was gone, but this time of year was not the right time to try to ask Dad anything. He was *way* too busy to think of his own potential happiness when he had to satisfy the needs of the entire population.

"I'll light it, shall I?" I nodded at the pit.

"No point, son. I need to get back to it, and if you don't mind..."

"I'll come help."

Standing up, he walked past me and patted my shoulder. "You're a good lad, *Nick*."

Dad was amused I'd changed my name but had said he understood my reasoning.

We worked for a large portion of the night before I made my excuses and went to bed, exhausted.

I was woken by a large banging at my... window? I looked outside to find Mya sitting on the top of the porch roof.

I'd gotten to know Mya while Dad and I had helped fix up the mansion she lived in with Death. She was a lot of fun and also a lot of... well, Mya.

I pulled up the sash window.

"Morning, Nicky Noo. I have a job for you." She tapped the side of her nose. "Secret squirrel and all that."

I rubbed at my eyes.

"You might want to get dressed, big boy. I mean there's no one passing the front of your establishment right now, and my eyes are only for one man, but..." She looked directly at my morning wood in my boxers. "*Hard* not to look."

I felt my cheeks flush.

"Hey, you look so like your daddy when you go red." She pointed, making me go redder still. It was too early for this shit.

"Mya, come around the back. I'll meet you in the yard in a few minutes when I'm more suitably dressed for the occasion."

"Will do. I'll put in a good word for you with Dela now too. Let her know the main tool in your toolbox is a superior model."

I pulled the window down and the curtains shut. Great, Mya knew about my crush. Bloody all of Gnarly would then soon.

I got washed and changed and with a steaming cup of much needed coffee, I came out the back to meet Mya.

"How do you know about my crush on Dela?" I asked her.

"Dude, you stare at her all the time like a panting dog in the heat. Might want to change your actions if you want to keep it a secret. There's no point though because the entire village must know unless they're blind."

"It's a waste of time anyway. She's not interested."

Mya patted my hand. "I'm not at liberty to go into the details, but Dela has had a lot on her mind lately. Family shit. Anyway, I've a proposition for you, and seeing as shortly I need to whizz off for Callie and Lawrie's wedding in Vegas, I need to get on with talking to you about it."

"Callie and Lawrie are getting married? Today?"

"Yup. So exciting. Anyway, this is what I need to

talk to you about. It's going to be my wedding present to them. I was thinking..."

Mya told me her plan and then she got up to leave. I thought about what my dad had said about Fenella. "Will you let Fenella know about the wedding? I'm sure she'll want to do something for the newlyweds."

"Will do, and thanks so much for helping with the pressie."

"No problem." Well, it might be. It could be a huge problem. But that was Mya's gamble, not mine.

After spending the morning consulting with the other people involved in organising the wedding present, I then was roped in by a very annoyed Jason to help rig up a huge projector in the boulevard so that we could watch the wedding live from Vegas.

To say it was short notice, Fenella had pulled out all the stops, setting up chairs just as if we were in the chapel facing us on screen. I watched as Callie passed her bouquet to Dela, who looked like Tinkerbell herself in her green dress with her gossamer wings on display. My heart beat faster and then once again I felt like I had a stone wedged in my stomach.

The ceremony started and we all sat, watched, and cheered as the happy couple said their vows.

Afterwards, the party in Gnarly started in earnest because the marriage was the *absolute* proof that the curse was lifted.

By the time I woke up Monday morning to start work on the wedding gift, I'd begun to regret how much I'd drunk the night before.

CHAPTER
THREE

Dela

I attempted to get out of Ginny's arms which was ridiculous really. Like a fly attempting to get out of a spider's web, or like an autumnal leaf attempting to stay on a tree in a hurricane.

"Let me go," I yelled, frustrated.

"Not until you calm down," Ginny insisted with a firm response, both verbally and physically. "You can't just stomp over there; you could get injured."

I allowed myself to go slack in her arms despite every cell in my body wanting to do the exact opposite.

"I'm going to let you go, but if you make one move over there before we've talked, I'll grab you again."

As she said it the ball swung at the building once more and detritus fell.

"But he's knocking down the café!"

"I'm well aware of what's happening and that it's clearly a shock to you. However, we need to get his attention and *then* find out what the heck is happening."

I grumbled. "It's okay for you being so calm. It's not your place. My sister told me to look after the building and LOOK AT IT. It barely exists. She will KILL ME."

Virginia quirked a brow. "I'm being so calm because I can see some of my clan standing around. Our builders. I think something planned is going on, we just need to find out what."

"Planned, schmanned. Callie would have told me." I looked over again as Nick stopped and peered over at the side of his crane, where Mya had now turned up. "Mya's here. She'll get to the bottom of what's happening."

I made my way over to Mya and Nick, my feet stomping against the ground because I was not okay right now. Ginny accompanied me, keeping close to my side like I was out on day leave from my asylum and she was my carer.

Mya looked over, saw me and grinned and then it all fell into place. This was Mya's doing.

"Why are you grinning at me, fang-face? Want to tell me why my apartment is now on the GROUND FLOOR in a jigsaw puzzle arrangement?" I put my hands on my hips. You could have run a spa around my ears because I was *steaming*.

"It's my secret wedding gift to the happy couple, pissy britches."

"You might have told me before knocking down my apartment," I yelled.

"You moved out! You live with the twins now. I sent all the rest of your stuff there. And can you keep your voice down. Most of us here have superior hearing."

I breathed out a long exhale. "You sent my belongings to the twins' place?"

"Of course. I'm not just going to destroy all your things. Gnarly would have me staked for not being environmentally friendly. We'll be using as much of these building materials as possible in the rebuild too."

I realised Nick was staring at me from his cab, his expression one of trepidation.

"The place will be rebuilt pretty fast, Dela, with

the vampire builders on board, so if you do want to move back in, it won't be long," he said, no doubt attempting to calm me down.

I ran my right hand through my hair, and ignoring Nick, I fixed my gaze firmly back on Mya. "So what's the wedding present then? I seriously hope you've not fucked up, knocking down her pride and joy."

"She'll be delighted. We were chatting when she thought she was dying and she said how much she'd have loved to have a café-come-bookstore. She called it *Books and Buns*, so that's what I'm creating here. It'll be extended to the side so double the original size floorplan, which also gives the newlyweds more space in the apartment above. New state-of-the-art kitchen equipment is being installed. I'm getting away with that by it being more energy efficient, and the interior will slightly dilute Callie's penchant for pink, so that Lawrie can work there without getting murderous. I'll work vampire black in. Black for a bookstore is perfection."

"Wow, you've thought of everything," I said witheringly.

Mya ignored my sarcasm and beamed.

"Aren't you going to be stupidly busy running a

bookstore alongside sorting out wayward souls?" I asked her. Mya had worked at a bookstore before she died and so I reckoned hadn't put this present together completely altruistically.

"Oh I can't run it."

I tilted my head as I stared at her. "So who's running the bookstore then?"

"Erm, you?"

I shook my head firmly. "Not a chance. I don't need to work, and I have no intention of being in front of newlyweds all day. No thanks."

"But she's your sister."

"You licked it first, the bookstore is yours."

"I can't run it. I have wayward souls to settle."

"I know someone who'll run it," Ginny interrupted. "But, Mya, you'll have to learn how to play nice, and you might have to run it past Gnarly's council. Back in a sec." Ginny disappeared.

Mya and I looked at each other and shrugged.

"Is there any chance you ladies can go chat somewhere else so that I can get on with this demolition?" Nick queried. "Only the sooner I've done that, the sooner our vamp friends can rebuild. They're a lot faster than I am."

"Well, we would usually converse in the cupcake

café, but oh look, there doesn't seem to be one any longer," I snapped.

Mya took my arm and dragged me in the direction of the park. "It's a nice day. We can have a walk while you get over your PMT."

"I don't have PMT."

"You do. Post matrimonial twatness. Your sister got married and you're pissed off because everything in her world is now shiny and bright and yours is the same as before."

"I'm single and she's married. I'm homeless and she's having a new house and shop built. Excuse me if I'm feeling a little sorry for myself right now." I huffed.

"We all have shit to bear, Dela. I died last year, but things worked out okay. Your sister was fated to die, things turned out okay. You're single and home-less right now, but I'm sure things will turn out fine. Anyway, I have a plan for you too." The next thing I knew, I'd been whizzed into the woodland that surrounded the park.

"What's the plan? To bury me here, so you don't have to hear me moan anymore?"

"Tempting," Mya said, sucking on her lower lip as if she might be reconsidering her original ideas. "But no. Look around you."

I did. There were some old, dead tree stumps and not much else.

"There's nothing much to look at in this actual spot. Do you mean look around at the whole woodland?"

"That's my point, Dela. The trees in this part of the wood contracted a disease. They got the rest of the woods treated quickly, but this space can't be replanted on. Now, the other side of the woodland is shifter territory, but this small space is, in my opinion, available. You fae love your woods right? You have money. Why don't you have a home built here? Nick and the vamps can build it for you."

"Nick and the vamps sounds like an EMO rock band," I said, while I looked around at the space. Could this really be where I lived? I imagined a log cabin situated among the woodland. Just for me for now, but then maybe at some point, for me and a significant other, and then a family. The thing I didn't have other than my sister—*family*. Callie and I had been adopted by humans, abandoned by our fae parents. Things had not gone well with our human parents and five years ago we'd become estranged, resulting in Callie and I moving to Gnarly Fell to start new lives. Perhaps living in the woods would make me feel more fae?

"So, what do you think?" Mya asked.

"I think I'm really considering it," I said.

"You are?"

I felt a strange feeling in my body. My stomach felt like butterflies fluttered within it. My heart beat faster. Goose bumps skittered up my arms, and then a great beaming smile cracked across my face, along with a tingle in my brain. A tingle of hope.

Callie had said for me to not contact any of our family until after she was dead, but she meant after she'd been murdered as was previously foretold. Not her fae death which would take hundreds of years. I would create a new family home and I would learn about my fae family, and if nothing else, glean information about my ancestry to teach my own children should I be fortunate enough to have any.

Oooh, that was also something I could do first. Have a child. No way could a fae have babies with a vampire. That was rarer than a person's survival on a soap opera. I needed a man for that though. One with good genetics. I'd have to get my dating life back in action imminently.

"Let's go back and discuss things with Nick and the vampire builders, then once the cupcake café is finished, they might be able to squeeze building you a home in. We need them to draw up some plans with you, to submit to the council."

"Do you think the council will say yes?" My voice sounded smaller, a sign my confidence was waning.

"Well, they meet on Wednesday evenings, and I'm sure Mr Stan Anderson who is on the council but under a lot of pressure right now, will be keen to stamp his approval on plans drawn up by his own son." She took hold of my arm. "Get ready, I'm whizzing us back."

I felt like I was on a spin cycle. Not only from Mya whizzing me back and forth, but from all the crazy activity. In just a week there'd been sister might be murdered, sister married, new café/bookstore, new potential home for me, and now I was thinking of contacting my fae family and finding my own baby daddy. I needed a drink, and not a non-alcoholic one.

And things were about to get even more complicated.

Ginny stood next to Aria. Now Mya and Aria were polite to each other, but Mya was not happy that Death and Aria had once dated. Not happy at all.

"Oh, hey, Aria. What brings you back to Gnarly so soon?" Mya enquired, trying to sound sweet. Unfortunately, Mya didn't do sweet, so it came out served with a side of vinegar.

"I'm going to run the bookstore," Aria announced. "I can't wait."

CHAPTER
FOUR

Nick

I decided to climb out of the cab when I saw that there were four women, including the one who'd organised this 'surprise' looking deep in conversation. I didn't want to do anything else until I found out why Mya had her hands on her hips, looking at the other two vampire women and shaking her head.

"...be someone from Gnarly," I heard Mya say.

"But it's my dream job. It's not fair. You got to do it when you were human. I was born a princess and never got to work a day in my life."

"Everything okay, ladies?" I said, my eyes naturally landing on Dela after I looked from Mya to the other woman. "Just want to check before I knock anything else down."

"Just talking about staffing the bookstore, that's all," Mya said. "The rebuild is all systems go still."

"Oh that's good. I'll get back on with it then."

"Actually, I want to talk to you about something," Dela said, and my heart beat faster in my chest. She did? Was she actually considering going out on a date with me? Had she changed her mind? "Are you able to take a break? We could head to the bistro for a spot of brunch?"

"Sure. Do you mind if I just pop home to clean up first?" I asked.

"You won't be long, will you? Only this build needs to happen as quickly as possible," Mya queried, breaking off from her own discussions.

"He gets a lunch break, right? We'll be back in an hour," Dela told her, and she cocked her head in the direction of our hardware store and set off walking.

I fell into step behind her. "You practicing for the Olympics or something? You're walking very fast."

"Glad to get away from the vampire women. They're always so... intense."

"What's the problem there? Mya looked pissed."

"Aria wants to run the bookstore, and it's hitting a tender spot with Mya, because Aria once dated Death."

"Ah. The old green-eyed monster."

"It's stupid because Aria is perfect for it. She loves books apparently. She rarely needs to sleep and so she can work there all the hours they need. She knows Lawrie well, as her husband is Lawrie's best friend. Mya needs to get over it. She's with Death now. Aria is married to someone else."

'Love rarely makes sense," I said, earning me a strange stare from Dela. I decided to change the subject. "So what did you want to talk to me about?"

"Mya just took me to a spot in the woods where there's enough space for me to have a house built. It would be perfect. I wondered if you'd look at it, draw me up some plans, and help me submit it to the council... who are meeting on—"

"Wednesday," I finished for her. I knew when they were meeting because my dad had been moaning that 'didn't they know he had enough to do this week without holding a council meeting'. So she didn't want to change her mind about coming on a date. I should have known really. I broke eye contact with her for a moment because I didn't want her to see the disappointment in my gaze.

"I realise it's short notice," she said, looking up at me. She licked her lips and her eyes seemed to glow. She was so... excited. I wished she would have looked at me that way when I'd asked her on a date. But I needed to not cut off my nose to spite my face. Helping her with this home would give me time with her. Hopefully enough time to convince her that I was the man of her dreams.

We reached my house. "Okay. I'll help you. I'll go grab a notebook and pen, so you can give me your ideas while we're in the bistro and then tonight are you able to meet me at the park and show me the site itself?"

"Absolutely." She grinned. "I'm so excited about the space, honestly. Mya said if we got you and the vamp builders on it, it would be done in no time."

I nodded my head. "The bookstore will be done by Wednesday. That's how fast they work. So if you get approval Wednesday evening, I reckon you could be in by Saturday and spend Christmas in your own new home."

Grabbing my arm, Dela squeezed. Then she seemed a little disconcerted as her fingers clutched my bicep. "Th-this is amazing," she said, and I pretended she meant my muscle and not her house plans. She quickly dropped her arms back down by her side.

We walked around the back of the store. "Right, you can come sit in the kitchen while I just get washed or you can sit out here." Dela was gazing around at the seated area near the fire pit.

"Wow. This is so beautiful." I watched as her head took in the house and the workshop. "I would hang fairy lights across here. It would be magical."

"Yeah, well, it's just me and my dad, and at this time of year we focus on making it magical for everyone else."

"Are you back to pretending he's Father Christmas again?" She laughed. "Go get cleaned up, or you'll not have time for lunch. Mya will come whizz you back to the café in the middle of eating."

I nodded and entered my home, feeling dejected once more that Dela did not seem to be able to see the spirit of Christmas all around her.

Shortly after I pushed through the doors of *Smokin' Hot*, the smell of barbecued meat began tantalising my nose. I'd started work early that morning and the sausage butty I'd begun the day with was a distant memory to my now rumbling tummy. Luckily, the Christmas music playing in the background covered the embarrassing gurgle. The bistro only usually opened in an evening, but Christmas week it opened lunchtime too. The place was packed out and I wondered if we were not going to be able to get a table, which would be hell now I'd smelled the delights.

A blonde wandered over. "I'm supposed to be turning people away, but I can squeeze you two in as long as you pick the day's special of surf and turf as we have those ready to go."

"Thanks, Chantelle. That's fine with me. What about you, Nick?"

"Sounds wonderful," I replied.

"Okay, let me show you to your seats," Chantelle said.

After we'd sat in the only remaining seats, at the back and near to the toilets, I placed my pad and pen on the newly cleaned table. "Lucky your friend was working today."

"Wasn't it? I don't know why everyone gets so worked up about Christmas," Dela said. "It's just one day of the year and yet mayhem starts from the moment bonfire night is over."

"You're not interested in it at all then? Not even when you were a child?"

"No." There was a hard edge to that simple one-word answer, and I wondered what had happened in her past. I waited a moment to see if she was going to elaborate further, but when no more words were forthcoming, I picked up my pen.

"Okay, tell me about your ideal living space and I'll do some general sketches. Once I've visited the site, I'll put together a proper plan."

Just like that the bitterness rolled off her face like a landslide clearing the side of a mountain, and an enthusiastic Dela launched into her dreams for her family home.

"Does it seem weird that I want to make a family place when I'm very single? Do you think I should make a smaller place?" she asked me afterwards while our drinks and meals were being brought to our table.

"No, it makes perfect sense for future planning. Both for if you have a family, or if you decide to leave Gnarly."

"I've no intention of leaving Gnarly. It's my home," she said, with a hint of ice in her voice.

"Hey, I feel exactly the same way about the place." I raised my hands up in a surrender motion.

"Sorry. It's just we were lucky enough to be allowed to be residents here, and it's the first place Callie and I really called home. Callie and Lawrie are staying here thank goodness, because I don't want to leave. I've settled here. As much as I like to go out into London in an evening, Gnarly is my *home*," she repeated, and she didn't realise but she placed a hand over her heart as she said it.

I remembered the first time I saw Dela. At first, I'd only seen Callie as she'd overseen the opening of her cupcake café, and then it had its grand opening and there she was. The petite strawberry blonde, whose hands trembled as she served the drinks and cupcakes while Gnarly residents fired their nosy questions at her like snowballs flew at fellow schoolkids the moment they left the safety of the school grounds. By the next day the nerves had gone, and she was laughing and joking with the Gnarly lot like she'd never lived anywhere else, but I remembered that Dela. The one who'd be unsure of herself, and I felt that version of Dela was still there, buried down just under the surface.

"You've lived here all your life, right?" she asked me.

"Well, since I was a few weeks old. My mum said she couldn't deal with a supernatural baby and so she left me with dad after I was born."

"So what exactly is your biology? What kind of creatures are you and your father? I can't work it out. I mean your dad hasn't changed in the five years I've known him, but you've aged a little."

"I'll age slowly and then once Dad decides to pack in, I'll take over. I'll become like him: ruddy faced and white haired. We're a distant relation of a Nephilim."

"That's human mum, angel dad?"

"Yeah. So the Nephilim, Nicholas, moved to live in the North Pole, and ceased to age. The residents there, the humans, treated him like a god. He had white hair and ruddy cheeks, but he never let them see his wings. They were so good to him, that he wanted to give back, so he set up an industry carving ornate wooden boxes. Elves lived nearby and their elder approached Nicholas and secured bed and board for his kin in return for helping to make the boxes. They handed them out to the villagers on December 25th and the villagers were so happy it became a tradition. But the idea spread. Not only did Nicholas give presents every December 25th but so did the villagers. Then people outside the village heard of the custom and that was that. Christmas. Nicholas had a family and the eldest boy eventually took on the role of Chief Gift Creator, but when it was handed down to my father, he didn't want to stay in the North Pole all year. He left his chief elf in charge over there and moved a small part of the business here. Now of course although they still carve a wooden gift for the people of the North Pole, there's now a huge logistical operation for delivering gifts."

Dela took a large drink of her wine.

"S- so your dad, really is F-Father Christmas?"

I nodded.

Looked like the girl finally got it.

CHAPTER FIVE

Dela

He'd not been bullshitting me. His father, Stan, really was Santa? Part of me still wanted to snort and say 'pull the other one' but why could it not be true? After all, I was a tooth fairy, which leant itself to the same principles of children believing in us. I guessed deep down I knew that the reason I didn't want to face it being the truth was because Callie and I had never had magical Christmases and I couldn't understand why we'd never experienced the magic of the season.

"Your Christmases must have been amazing," I said. "I mean the son of Santa himself."

Nick's smile didn't reach his eyes. "My father's job takes him away from home over the holiday season, or he's busy in the workshop."

"Oh," I said as realisation struck me. "So he doesn't get to celebrate with you?"

"I stayed with Fenella and Jason for Christmas Day every year, because dad was away with work, until I was old enough to decide to stay on my own, and even then, I always went over there for the amazing dinner Fen cooked. I'm sure you can imagine she pulled out all the stops to make it amazing. Still, it's not the same when you're without your own family."

I stared at my glass and rubbed at the condensation on it. "Oh you can be around family and it still not be the same. Not if they decide they're not celebrating Christmas. That it's a consumerist belief, removed from the original meaning of the birth of Christ."

I could feel Nick's eyes boring into me and eventually I gave in and looked up to meet them.

"My dad always made sure we celebrated on Boxing Day, but he was so tired. He'd get up and do the whole present thing dressed up in his suit and then an hour later he'd be fast asleep on the sofa. He's an amazing father, always has been, but there have been times I've been incredibly lonely. I'm just very lucky I had Jason and his mum in my life. At least you always had your sister."

"True. I don't know what I'd have done without Callie. If she'd have died last week..."

Nick startled. "What? Did something happen to Callie?"

I found myself explaining the last week's strangeness to this person who before today I'd barely spoken to. Conversation seemed to flow easily between us, and we seemed to understand each other. But I hoped this didn't get his hopes up for me to agree to a date with him because my rules still applied. I would only date outside of the village. I couldn't risk spoiling my home.

"Wow. Mya said you'd had a lot on your plate lately. I had no idea."

"How could you? But let's just say I could really use having my own place because what with all Callie's drama and now the café being demolished and rebuilt, I feel unsettled."

"You need roots and we'll get you some." Nick smiled and we went back to talking about my new home.

When we'd finished eating, Nick headed back to the ruins of the café and I went to *Seconds the Best* to catch up with the twins.

"Dela," they said in unison as I pushed through the entrance of their second-hand store.

I noticed that Tilly raised her brow at Milly and after receiving a nod she spoke, *on her own.* "The wedding looked incredible."

"You looked beautiful," Milly added as she twirled a few strands of her blonde hair around her finger.

"You did. Well, everyone did," Tilly said.

I appraised one then the other. "Am I right in my assumptions that you are both taking care to speak separately?"

"Yes," they said together and then Tilly gestured for Milly to speak.

"We're trying to practice being less... twin. Now we can find love we need to separate ourselves slightly because we had an in-depth conversation and sharing a man is not for us."

"I think you've just decimated the dreams and fantasies of most of the male population in Gnarly and some of the females too," I quipped. "However, I think it sounds a good idea. It won't hurt for you to have a little independence from the other one. You can't possibly like all the same things all the time."

"We usually do. But maybe that's because we've always done everything together and if we spend some time discovering ourselves separately we might start having different interests?" Tilly said.

"Maybe so. But take your time. Learning to speak separately is a good start and then perhaps I could go to the bistro with one of you and then go to Zumba with the other, and then the week after do it the other way around?"

"But I might miss something off the specials menu if we go separately," both twins said together, and then they laughed at each other. "Twins," they called and linked their little fingers.

I was getting a headache. Today had been too full on. It was time to head back to their house and spend a few hours on my own until I met Nick again later in the park.

"Mya said she sent my stuff through to your place. Did it arrive okay?"

Again, the twins looked at each other for a beat and an eyebrow raise.

"Yes, it's all in your room waiting for you. Of course, there's now not much space in your room. Can barely get the door open in fact." Tilly pulled a grimace.

"Don't worry, it's not for much longer. I really appreciate all you two have done, letting me stay with you this past week and beyond, but I'm meeting Nick tonight—"

The twins both clapped. "At last, you have seen he's the one for you," they said.

"Erm, no. He's drawing up some plans for my own place. I'm hoping to be in for Christmas Day, so thank you for everything, but hopefully you will have your place back soon."

"Right, your own place," Milly said.

"That's what we meant to say," Tilly added.

"I'm not dating anyone who lives in Gnarly. You know this." I sighed.

"But he's so..." Milly shrilled.

"...fit," Tilly finished.

"Doesn't matter. His postcode is a problem for me. Right, I'd better get on my way. I'll see you both later."

"Bye," both replied.

I was the only person in Gnarly who knew the truth of the twins' background. Their 'family', a coven of witches, had run the *Seconds the Best* shop for generations. Unbeknown to her mother, a young witch had carved the twins out of wood as voodoo dolls in the likeness of her twin school-friends with whom she had quarrelled. Before use, the schoolfriends had been forgiven their misdemeanours and the dolls had laid in a toy chest for many years.

When the family decided to leave Gnarly, the witch's own daughter, who was the seventh generation of her family, had spelled the dolls to come to life, given she was incredibly strong. But she could only give the twins limited knowledge and so they appeared odd to others in Gnarly. It wasn't their fault. They'd been brought to life and abandoned by the family who'd created them, relying mainly on each other. They believed that their shared communication came from being created from the same piece of charmed wood. The witches had left the deeds of the shop to the twins who they'd named Milly and Tilly Wood.

But I knew that every day the twins feared that they might turn back into the wooden dolls they'd started life as because they didn't know the longevity or background of the spell that had created them in the first place.

Knowing that, it was easy to see why the twins found it hard to be separate from each other, and the curse of Gnarly had meant they'd really not had to worry about that too much, concentrating instead on their store. But love was a magnetic force that even the twins couldn't resist. The chance at a happy ever after.

By the time I'd finished daydreaming about the twins, I'd reached their house. Unlocking the front door with my spare key, I entered the hallway of their home. Inside the twins' house it was decorated with lots of mismatched furniture and furnishings from the store, but somehow it all pulled together into a boho/vintage style that worked. The fireplace and shelves held many ornaments, and the walls were full of assorted pictures. The sofas were piled with cushions and throws, and the floors had rugs, but the sisters kept the furniture to a minimum in the main rooms, so although it held a lot there was still space to walk around comfortably.

Well in most rooms, I thought as I attempted to push open the door to my guest bedroom. I could only just get through the door. Any less space and I would have had to shrink myself into fairy me, something I had a fear of in case I couldn't switch back to a normal height. I'd never in all my life even attempted it, despite my elder sister's assurances that I'd be okay. I didn't trust the process given we'd had no fae to tell us our history. Callie had poured over books from libraries and antique bookstores. I'd preferred to pour over Tinder and Match.

Everything I owned was now in this small room. There wasn't a lot. A wardrobe and chest of drawers and some boxes containing my personal effects. It wasn't a lot to show for my twenty-seven years, but then again, was life about your material worth or the legacy you left behind? Huh, I was screwed in both directions. That said, there was something about the putting down of roots in this new house that made me feel that it was the start of something good. A gut feeling that life was going to suddenly reveal my true purpose.

Dela, it's just endorphins, you tit, I admonished myself. Still, I cleared a space on my bed, dropped down onto it and spent some time dreaming of what might be in my new home.

Nick: I'm running late. Want to come meet me at the store instead, and we can walk to the park together?

We'd swapped numbers in case of such changes of plan and so I quickly texted back.

Dela: Sure. On my way now.

Nick: Great. Call me old-fashioned but

I'd rather you didn't head into the park on your own at night anyhow.

Dela: I'm going to live in the woods you dick.

Nick: Oh, er yeah, sorry.

Dela: Sorry I called you a dick.

Fuck. Now I was thinking about dick because I'd typed the words. I'd bet Nick had a really decent trousersnake because he was so buff, but then again, maybe he was all lumberjack man because he compensated for a weeny weiner? I shook my head. I must not be thinking of Nick's dick.

Nick's dick wasn't very thick, but he made it work cos he knew a little trick.

Dela. For goodness' sake! Sometimes my mind ran away with me. Again, I blamed my human parents because they'd not taught us nursery rhymes and so I used to make up my own, based on the snippets I'd heard, or I redid ones I did pick up.

Jack and Jill went up the hill, to fetch a pail of water.

Jack fell down and broke his crown and forgot he had a daughter.

Bitter? Me?

After fixing myself a quick sandwich and eating it along with a packet of beef crisps, I walked from the twins' house over to Stan's. It meant I actually walked past the park, but Nick was doing me a favour and so if he wanted to meet me at his house, that's what I would do.

Heading around the back, I saw Stan himself come out of the workshop. He stood stock still for a moment and as he did his eyes flashed bright red. He let out a wicked "Mwah ha ha," and followed it up by saying, "Christmas is going to be hell." Then an elf came out to ask him something, so I quickly hid down behind the wall. I waited until I heard his footsteps move away and the door open, and then I walked back around, my heart thudding in my chest at what I'd just witnessed, but my inquisitive nature, ie being a nosy bitch, making me look again.

Stan was about to walk into his house.

"Dela," he said, followed by a broad smile. "Nick was telling me about your hopes for a place in the woods. I'll be sure to do my best to get it through on the council for you Wednesday evening."

"Th-thanks so much," I said. "I know you're busy."

"Yeah, being Father Christmas is no easy job, but it brings a lot of happiness."

I got brave. "I should imagine it can be busy as *hell*."

He shrugged. "I'm used to it. Done it for years now. But still, it'll be time to hand it over to Nick at some point. Once he's made some grandchildren to continue the line that is."

He'd not flinched at all at the word hell. I pushed on.

"Does it not get you down at times? I'd bet Satan himself wouldn't want to be around that many bratty kids in one go."

"Even the naughtiest of children experience the magic of Christmas, Dela." His brow furrowed. "Are you all right? You don't seem to be entering into the spirit of the season."

"Not every kid gets a Christmas though, do they? For some kids Christmas is painful, like a pit of fiery eternal torture," I told him, wondering if I was over-doing the hell aspect.

At that point Nick came to the door. "Sorry for the delay, Dela. I'm ready now. See you later, Pops."

"Yeah, catch you later," he said, looking at me strangely.

I didn't know whether it was because of what I'd said about Christmas being painful or whether it was about my repeated mentioning of hell, but one thing I was sure of... I'd seen Santa turn evil, and now I was even more convinced that though he might well be Santa, I was sure he was Satan too.

CHAPTER SIX

Nick

As I passed my father and he nodded his head at me in farewell, I noted the crease between his brows that came not from his weathered and loved Santa features, but from concern. Something had happened while Dela had talked with him, but I'd have to ask him later. Right now, it was time to go and draw up plans for Dela's dream home, and to put into action my own plans. Which were to win Dela over and get her to break her stupid rules about not dating anyone from the fell.

I'd had a little time to think things through while back at home, and if I spent time with her, getting to know her, and her me, then it'd kind of be dating by stealth. Before she knew it, I'd be in her life, and she'd not be able to let me go. That's how it went in my head anyway. Sometimes being born a soppy romantic had its disadvantages. I blamed a father who worked miracles and being around Fen who loved to sit us in front of Disney movies as kids, despite the fact we asked to watch *Star Wars*.

I knew I'd make the most amazing Prince Charming for someone. Oh my, the idea struck me as if Walt Disney himself had thrown a bolt of happy-ever-after lightning at my head. I'd use what I'd seen in the movies, and romance Dela until she fell madly in love with me just like the princesses fell for their princes! And I knew exactly how to start.

"I didn't have you down as the strong, silent type, so have you lost your voice?" Dela asked me and I realised I'd been so up in my head that I'd failed to talk since apologising for the delay in me leaving the house, (which was because I'd got changed multiple times in order to hopefully look attractive to Dela).

"Sorry, Dela. I'm already thinking up potential ideas, just suggestions of course, for your new place. We want to make sure it has everything you need. It's part of the tradesman in me. I can't help but get enthusiastic about new projects."

"You're not an architect though, are you? Don't I need one of those?"

Way to make a guy feel good about himself, I

thought, and one going out of his way to help her at that. I felt my face muscles tighten a little. "The vampires have architects. All we have to come up with tonight are some preliminary sketches and then they'll turn them into a detailed plan within an hour. Seriously, if the world could know vampires existed, new housing would be done in no time."

"Humans would not be able to cope. Technology and wanting-it-all has them all to cock and seeing the doctor for stress as it is." Dela sighed. "It's all in the women's magazines I read. There's a reason us supernaturals stay hidden in plain sight, and that's because of our ultimate sacrifice to care for the weak humans who outnumber us because they're more fertile. I learn so much from magazines. They have many thought-provoking articles, especially on mental health and wellbeing."

I thought it better to not mention this month's *Loaded* magazine that I'd bought which had Amy Childs from *Towie* on the cover clad in sexy black lingerie while she toyed with a piece of her red hair and looked up coyly at the camera. It wasn't my mental health that cover had taken care of that was for sure.

So instead I just went with, "That's true. And

you lived with humans, so you'd know first-hand about what they'd be like with supernaturals."

Dela uttered an embittered laugh. "They couldn't cope at all. We weren't allowed to demonstrate any of our fae abilities. They would have never let us know we even had them, but for the fact things happened that they couldn't ignore."

"Things?"

"Our wings."

"Ah."

We reached the entrance to the park which meant we had about another ten minutes to go before we'd get to the housing plot. "Tell me more about your childhood, Dela. If you want to, that is."

"Promise to keep it to yourself? I don't speak of either of my families because some in Gnarly are just too nosy, and this is my place of peace."

"I promise. Like I said, I get it. I don't discuss my mother either."

"Well, if you want to talk to me about it, you can. It's the least I can do, be an ear for you with everything you're doing for me."

Oh, she did realise I was putting myself out for her after all. A lot of people in Gnarly called Dela selfish, said she always put herself first. I hoped it was a defence mechanism and wanted to know her better to find out. The fact she was willing to tell me about her family and hear about mine was a great start. "Thanks. You first though. You'd already started saying that your human parents didn't want you showing that you were fae?"

She kicked away a stone in her path. It skittered off into the grass. "I don't know exactly why our fae parents gave us to Tom and Erica Francis, but they did when Callie was two and I was almost a year old. Neither of us remember anything about our real parents, but as we got older, we knew we were different because we were told to put our wings away. That people would be bad to us if they saw them. Would hurt us. If we ever did accidentally show them, it was passed off as fairy tale dress up."

"That must have been very confusing to you?"

"We were treated like we were bad if we showed our true selves, and we didn't understand that. We wanted to know our heritage, but all talk of that was shot down. Our parents were very strict and also believed children should be seen and not heard. They did nothing terrible, as in, we were fed and clothed and to a certain extent loved; but we were loved as human children and resented for what we actually were, and that's what finally fractured our family apart. Just over five years ago we asked for details of our fae parents and were told by Tom and Erica that if we went ahead and embraced being fae, they didn't want to see or hear from us again."

"What? That's crazy." I didn't understand how a parent—be it natural, fostered, or adopted—could turn their back on their child, but it had happened to me too.

"The fae had given them the children they'd always desired, but they believed our getting in touch could have the fae re-enter their lives and they didn't want that. So if we pursued it, we had to do it on our own. They said they'd done their job and brought us up to adulthood and now we were on our own. But if we ever changed our minds and went down the route of living as humans again, we knew where they were. It's bizarre. They only want us in their life if we show up as the human children their family and friends think we are. But that isn't who we are."

"And that's when you came to Gnarly?"

"Yes. We were told that we were tooth fairies and given the name of the woman who had brought us to Tom and Erica. Sheridan came to us almost immediately when we contacted her and shared all we needed to know about our ancestry in terms of what tooth fairies did and then she helped us get set up in Gnarly. We'd been born in the woodland here, though apparently our parents had only been passing through and weren't resident here. She said if we ever wanted to meet our fae parents to let her know, but we said no. Callie and I had talked and we wanted the chance to learn who we were and get settled in a home where we could be who we wanted. Only now I'd like to know who our real parents are whereas Callie still doesn't want to know."

"But Callie can't make that decision for you, can she? I get it could have repercussions for the both of you, but you have a right to know."

We'd reached the clearing and Dela walked in and sat down on a tree stump. I hovered nearby. "I want to know my background, Nick. It's okay for Callie. She's happily married now and feels settled. I have this churning feeling within me. It's the not knowing. I honestly don't think I can fully settle down until I know who I am, even if I build my dream house." She stared up at me, her eyes having widened. "Fuck, Nick, that's the truth. That's why I'm like I am. Until I know everything, I'm always going to feel I don't fully belong anywhere."

"Then find out. I'll help you. I'll come with you. And maybe in return, you'll help me contact my mother."

"You want to do that?"

I nodded. "But before we get into that. Let's get these plans done, so I can get them over to the vamps, and then submitted to the council."

"Okay," Dela said, but I could tell her previous exuberance about her new home had been tempered down now she'd realised it wouldn't provide all the answers to her feeling like she belonged.

"Okay, so three bedrooms including a master suite with views out the back looking over the woodland. That's going to be so relaxing. Now, let's talk about the en suite." I pointed to the floor where I'd sprayed temporary chalk paint to mark the areas out so she could see the floorplan as it would be. We stepped into the 'en suite room' and I discussed a huge window, again looking out over the back, but with windows that saw out but were blackened looking in so she could bathe under the stars with no peeping toms watching.

"Wow, yes, that would be amazing. And it needs to be a huge bath."

"You have the space for that."

All of Dela's plans for the house were for future

Dela. I understood. This was to be her home and she hoped eventually there would come a partner and children and she wanted room for that. But what was here for the Dela of now? I tried to get her thinking of what she wanted presently.

"Okay, so back to the bedroom." I raised a brow in a suggestive manner as we walked back into the space.

Dela grinned. "Looks like you've got me into the bedroom after all, Mr Anderson. Alas, not in the way you might have been hoping."

"Can't blame a guy for trying." I shrugged before winking.

She laughed, but then her expression turned serious. "You get my rule though, don't you?"

"I do. Even if I think your rule sucks. But given how you've found a place to call home, I totally get why you wouldn't want to do anything to ruin it."

"I just wanted to be clear that it's not you, it's me," she elaborated.

"Oh I know that. You have seen me, right?" I lifted my right arm and flexed a bicep.

"You're a great catch, Nick. I'm just not casting my net in Gnarly. However, if you'd like to move..."

I shook my head. "The right woman for me needs to take me as I am. And that is as a resident of

Gnarly Fell who is in waiting to become Father Christmas eventually. They need to want a large family and to understand that around the festive season they can either heartily take on the role of Mrs Claus, or they need to understand my job takes me away. Anyhow, let's not discuss how amazing I am any longer, and get back to this floorplan. If you take a look at this space here, we could make you an enormous closet for you to fill with beautiful dresses, so that if you need to get ready for a lovely evening out, well, my dear, you can go to the ball."

Her nose wrinkled up. "I'm not someone who gets dressed up a lot. That's mainly Callie's department, but I guess a large closet is a great idea because my future husband might have a lot of clothes, might he? So yes, let's put in an amazing closet."

I chalked up the outline for it and then changed tack, mentioning the downstairs area that I was spraying in blue chalk paint. You have a lot of room downstairs; you could have an amazing library like Belle in *Beauty and the Beast*."

"Never seen it, but I think the space would be best left un-shelved. Might become a family room. I can always add a bookshelf later."

"Do you not read?"

She shook her head. "Only the odd magazine or

crime book, but Mya has the whole turret library and my sister's about to gain a bookstore, so even if my reading increased, I don't think I need to be hoarding books too."

She had a point, but it meant my creating her fairy tale home wasn't working in the slightest.

In the end I gave up on suggesting things beyond the usual future family home and instead I let myself be directed by Dela. In the end we had sketches that covered everything needed, including a nice garden edged by where the still healthy trees stood. Hopefully the fungus that had felled the trees didn't affect grass.

"I'll hand these to the vamps in the morning. Oh, actually..." I trailed off.

"What?"

"I wondered if you would come and oversee things design wise at *Books and Buns*. Only my fear is of Mya abandoning this project partway through. You know your sister better than anyone. It'd be great if you'd check what we're doing and let us know if we can make any tweaks."

"Sure. It's the least I can do after you've been so kind. Plus, if my sister gets home and she doesn't have an improved business and living premises, but instead there's a gothic bookstore, Mya's going to be in her own The Book of the Dead again. So, what time do you want me there?"

"Is eight am too early?"

"I'll make myself a good flask of coffee. It's a date," she said. "Oops, not a date, it's a—"

"I'm clear of what it is. I'll see you at eight. Let me walk you back to the twins' house."

I could see she was about to protest, but then she closed her mouth and instead nodded and fell into step beside me.

CHAPTER SEVEN

Dela

I'd just been about to say once more that I was perfectly capable of walking to the twins' place, but I'd already noted the smile that had slipped off his face when I'd begun to correct my saying of the word 'date', and felt I'd better give the guy a break. There was also the fact he'd let me spill my guts to him about my human parents, and I'd said I'd repay the favour with him speaking of his mother.

Not only did I want to hear about his mum, but I wanted to ask him more about being brought up by his dad. See if there were any clues to potential satanic aspects of his upbringing. Oh boy! That would mean Nick was potentially part-demon too! I'd keep a watch for clues.

"I appreciate you walking me back. I'm just so

used to being independent, I find it hard to let go of it. You see, I didn't want Callie to think when we left home, that she had to parent me, so I went out of my way to assert my being free and liberated."

"Whereas I was brought up by a male role-model who is kind to all. Therefore, caring for others, love, and kindness is at the root of who I am. Some people think that makes me weak, but I actually believe it's the opposite." Then Nick screamed and jumped, wafting at his arm. "What was that? Ahhhh. Do I have a spider on me? Check me for spiders, Dela, quickly. Ugh. Oh my god, I knew I'd get one on me being in the woods."

I stood giggling. I couldn't help myself. Nick was dancing around while knocking imaginary spiders off his body. It looked like the worst kind of dad dancing.

"It's not funny. I hate them. Is there one? I beg you, check me, and get it off me."

"Nick. I'd patted your arm, when you said people felt it made you weak, being caring. I'm so sorry, I didn't know it would make you freak out thinking you had a spider on you." Once again I laughed, to the point I had to clutch my stomach.

"I don't know how you can be so okay, being out in the woods, with all those creepy-crawlies around."

He shuddered. It looked so strange, seeing a big hunk of a guy being creeped out over crawlies. Reminded me we shouldn't make assumptions on first impressions.

"Aw, mate. I appreciate you spent time in the woods with me to draw up the plans when you're so scared of..." I moved closer and ran my fingers up his arm. "Spiders."

He grabbed hold of my hand to pull it off me. "Stop that at once, you torment," he said.

His baby-blue eyes met mine and his lips parted. He'd said torment as I'd teased him, but now I knew he felt I was tormenting him in another way entirely. By not pursuing anything between us. My small and dainty hand was encased within his big bear like one and I could feel the roughness of his worker's palm as I moved mine out of his grip.

"I promise to protect you from arachnids, okay? Just don't swat out at anything winged if you can help it, because if I learn to shrink myself it could be me." I decided a swift change of subject was in order. "Now, tell me about your mum. What do you know about her?"

After a beat of silence, Nick began to walk again. "Just that she was human. My dad met her in London at a club and had a 'dalliance' as he called it.

They dated for a short while but when he tried to tell her he was Father Christmas she thought he was crazy and broke things off.

"He'd told her where he lived in case she ever changed her mind and went home thinking the curse of Gnarly had struck again, which it may have done, but I think it's far more likely that my mother at that time thought he was crazy. And then one day she showed up with me. Her face had been white as a sheet as she'd told my father she'd entered my room to find elves there who'd left carved gifts at the foot of my cot. She said she wanted no part of a supernatural life where strange creatures could just appear in her home."

"Maybe she just freaked out? I mean anyone would."

"My dad considered that. He attempted to get in touch with her a few more times as I was growing up, but she still didn't want to know. The final time he went, when I was five, she'd met and married another guy, a human guy, and had had a baby. A healthy baby with no weird family. He didn't seek her out after that. She'd made her choice."

"That's awful. To turn your back on the son you birthed. I hope her other kid grew up to be a huge brat who drove her crazy. I mean that kid would be twenty-five now, right? With any luck he ended up in prison."

Nick laughed at that, and I smiled, pleased I'd brought something other than a frown to his features.

"One can only hope." He laughed again.

"Ooh, has Nick got a little bit of a naughty streak inside him?" I teased, hoping to tempt out any hidden demon.

"If Nick has, you're not getting to know. That side of me comes out in the bedroom, and you, lady, are friend-zoned."

We reached my door.

"Eight am, on what most definitely is not a date," he said. "Night, Dela."

He turned away and walked down the path, giving me a final wave before he went out of sight.

Tonight I'd got to know Nick a whole lot better, and although my home plans had become clearer, my inner turmoil seemed to have just gotten worse.

Because I liked him, but I couldn't let things go any further regardless.

CHAPTER EIGHT

Mya

"**W**here on earth have you been? We already took time off for the wedding and Gnarly's celebration. Now you need to be sorting out wayward souls, Mya."

"You can be a real party pooper at times," I complained to my boyfriend.

"I'm Death. I've pooped at many, many parties as either the host or a guest has decided to depart the party early and I've been given the role of designated driver to their final destination."

I began to giggle. "You've pooped at parties?"

Death sighed a long, drawn-out sigh. "You know what I meant. I didn't think before I said it."

Closing the distance between us, I patted him on the arm. "Calm down, Big D, I'm here now, ready and able to work long into the night. I've been busy arranging Callie and Lawrie's wedding gift."

"How long can it take to order a set of saucepans?"

'Oh, I decided against that," I informed him. "Instead, I decided to knock down the cupcake café and have it rebuilt into a baked goods shop come bookstore."

Death immediately took his phone from his pocket and swept his fingers across. "You're not destined to die. Then again, your best friend doesn't know about this development yet. I think we should go to bed and make the most of what time we have left." His dark eyes danced with mischief. I loved it when he got naughty.

"What about all the wayward I've neglected?" I teased.

"Oh, I'm sure another hour or so won't make that much of a difference," he said, and then he picked me up and whisked me to our bedroom.

Death wasn't so *cocky* the next morning when I called him to say I had one less wayward than I should have.

"We need to check the app and The Book of the Dead again and then contact Heaven and Hell to see if one was shipped there. Could be that at the last minute they did something good or bad that tipped the scales. It's happened before. Rare but not impossible," Death reassured me.

But despite checking, rechecking, and consulting the departments above and below, we remained a wayward short.

I opened The Book of the Dead.

"Wayne Everly, aged thirty-two. Dead through smoke inhalation. He set homemade Christmas decorations on fire purposefully and put his ex-wife in hospital. Luckily his children had been at their maternal grandmother's house."

"We've got to find him. He shouldn't be able to leave the mansion."

At that point Jenny appeared. The ex-librarian and the witch who'd placed and then lifted the curse on the village, lived at the mansion with Spence, a ghost pirate. She'd known the Death before mine, and that and her knowledge from the books of Gnarly made her a great source of information at times.

"The only way a spirit can leave the mansion is if their fate will be decided outside of it," she declared.

"But the wayward end up here in Gnarly. Nowhere else," Death said. "Don't they?" he asked, no longer sounding so certain.

"Indeed, and so he's still in Gnarly," Jenny agreed. "For some reason he's not been bound to the Home of Wayward Spirits though but allowed into Gnarly itself. Now all Mya has to do is find him and work out whether he's for heaven or hell."

"What do you mean, I have to *find* him?" I placed my hands on my hips. "Can't I just call him to me? I'm a super powerful Death-touched vampire queen."

"No, you'll actually have to go looking for him. And an escaped spirit can be a tricky prospect because they wrongly assume they're escaping their fate by being able to body hop."

"Body hop? You mean there's a wayward out there possessing people? Why didn't you tell me this was possible earlier this morning?" I narrowed my eyes at her. "Also, did I let this person escape, or were you and Spence too busy in his bedroom and not watching what was going on here while we were at the wedding?"

"You can talk. We left our room to try to quieten the wailing spirits last night only to discover it was you."

"Ladies," Death interrupted. "We all need to work together here. There's potentially an evil demon-to-be loose in Gnarly Fell."

I swallowed. Had I caused this by not being here to do my job properly? And what if Callie didn't like the bun and bookstore? Business owners usually made their own ideas on expansion, didn't they?

What had seemed like amazing ideas yesterday: presents and penis, had in the cold light of day begun to leave me wondering if I'd made the right choices.

"So I have to spend time in Gnarly on the lookout for an escaped spirit, on top of keeping processing the backlog and incoming wayward?" I double-checked with Jenny.

"Yes, but of course you can't let anyone in the fell know there's an escapee or you'll cause chaos. They are all rather sensitive creatures and also they don't allow new people into the village without an in-depth analysis, remember?"

"Let it go, Jenny. You're past all that now and loved up with Spence."

She nodded. "Who I shall return to now. I've told you everything I needed to. Happy hunting."

With that she left the room wearing a very smug expression, not unlike the one she'd used to have upon her face when we'd both aimed for a customer at the bookstore where we used to work in London and she'd pinched them from under my nose.

"Looks like I have quite the to-do list today," I said to Death. "And you are definitely not on it. No distracting me with your Big D until I've sorted this backlog and found the spirit."

"I have souls to collect today, so I will be out of your hair," Death announced.

"We both know it's bare down there," I quipped, receiving an eye roll in return, but I also noted the slight uptick at the corner of Death's mouth.

My eyes flickered into his Big D area. Was it me or was he packing today? All was revealed when he reached into his pocket and drew out rolled up paper. "My to-do list," Death explained.

"Babe, you've got to start using notes on your phone. Gnarly won't be happy at the wasted paper."

"It recycles."

I fixed him with a look. "Got to keep up with the kids, Big D."

He pulled out his phone from his other pocket and then as he swiped across the screen, his eyes widened and his hand shook so much his phone dropped to the floor and bounced across what was thankfully a very thick rug under the table, so it survived unscathed.

"What is it? Please tell me Callie is not fated to die again?"

He shook his head, pulling a chair out from under the kitchen table and plonking himself down on it.

"No, Mya. It says Stan will die today. *Father Christmas* is going to die."

Pulling out the chair opposite, I fell into the other one.

Father Christmas could NOT die.

Nick

Once home, I kicked off my shoes, grabbed a beer and slumped onto the sofa. It had been a long day and my feet ached. There was no sign of my dad, but I knew with days to go until the big day I wouldn't see much of him outside of the workshop.

Was he really waiting for me to settle down and have kids and then hand over the reins? I knew it must be wearing, knowing every December you had the responsibility of Christmas hanging over you, but I wanted to be around my kids at Christmas, which I could do if Grandpa remained Santa. I huffed then. Why was I even thinking about it? I was as far away from being settled down as you could get. I decided there and then that I would give myself until New

Year's Eve to try to get Dela to change her mind and then after that, my resolution would be to forget her and date other women.

I made myself a quick supper of toast and jam and washed it down with a cuppa having abandoned the beer. I made my way upstairs after ensuring my sketches were safely in my backpack. Deciding a bath was just the thing for my aching legs and feet, I soaked in the tub for an hour and then after drying off went to bed where I fell asleep dreaming of spiders attacking me in the woods. By the time I woke up, my bedcovers were on the floor, no doubt from me fighting off imaginary creepy crawlies.

"You really should close your curtains at night," a voice said, making me jump. I looked at the window where Mya was perched outside it once again.

"And close the windows to keep pesky vampire queens from disturbing my peace." I reached for my pillowcase and placed it across my crotch. "What is it you're wanting, Mya?" I asked her.

She pulled my window up further. "I just wanted to let you know that I won't be around at the bun and bookstore today. Only, I've got an important wayward job to deal with. Very important, highly secretive task. Basically, it's like I'm in the MI5 or something. I cannot possibly discuss it. It's a 'The name's Bond, Mya Bond' kind of thing."

For someone who couldn't talk about it, she was uttering a lot of words.

"That's fine. I asked Dela if she'd come and oversee things and she agreed. She's meeting me at the building at eight."

"Oh. Well, that's fantastic. I can carry on with my super important task then and…" Mya stopped then and looked like she wanted to say something but the words wouldn't quite form. Eventually she ground out, "Sorry, did you say Dela had offered to help you? Because that's highly unusual."

"I asked her last night. I'm helping her with her new house and in return she's going to make sure we get this right for her sister."

"Ah, so it's a 'you scratch my back, I scratch yours' kind of arrangement? Like, her eyes haven't turned red lately or anything, have they?"

"What?" I grimaced. It was too early for Mya's general exuberant weirdness.

"Nothing, nothing."

"Why would her eyes turn red?"

"Erm, if she'd been erm, crying or something. Yes, she might have been upset, you know after all the 'her sister almost died' stuff. Anyway, as you were. Well, not as you were because you were showing me your dick, but you may carry on with your day. Byeee."

She disappeared and I rubbed at my chin. After enduring Mya first thing upon waking I needed about three cups of tea to recover, so I quickly got dressed.

Making my way downstairs, I heard pots clattering in the kitchen and found my dad had just brewed a pot of tea. He looked past me, making me turn around.

"Is she coming down?" he asked me.

"Who?"

"I heard a woman's voice. Thought you might have brought Dela home."

Huh, I wished that was the case.

"Nope. Just Mya on the outside of the house again. This time letting me know that she had wayward business and so wouldn't be around the build."

"Oh, that's a shame, son."

"No it's not, she just distracted us all yesterday anyway."

"I meant Dela not being upstairs. Did the date go well though?"

"No, Dad. It wasn't a date. I was helping her draw up plans for her new home, remember?"

"Aw, I was hoping she'd see sense. See how virile my son was. Do you mean to tell me the only wood that got any attention was the felled trees?"

"I'm not going to discuss my private life with you, except to say there is no me and Dela. We're just friends."

"Friends, huh? Well before yesterday I wouldn't have said you were even that, so it's a step in the right direction, isn't it, son?" He passed me a mug of tea. The illustration on the mug was a man clutching his privates and the words: *I said deck the **h**alls, woman* was written above it.

I changed the subject. "You straight back into the workshop?"

"Indeed. Lots to do."

"Do you need me to cancel my—"

Dad shook his head vigorously. "No. You've the bookstore and hopefully the house build if the plans go through tomorrow. If that gives Dela and Callie their places to settle down, then you'll have created a Christmas miracle of your own; especially with Dela. That girl made out she'd never had a good Christmas earlier. That needs rectifying. This one needs to be incredible for her. Enough to make up for all the ones that didn't measure up. You up for that, son? Call it a trainee task. Give Dela the most amazing Christmas." He paused. "Even if you gain nothing in return."

"I'll do my best, Dad."

"It's all you can do, son. Righto, I'm going to fill my flask and go see what the elves managed overnight."

He made his way over to the door.

"Dad?"

"Yeah?" He looked back at me, and a crease came to his brow. "You okay?"

"I want to see Mom." My words surprised the both of us.

"You do?"

"I, well, I think so. I'm considering it. I know she'll probably not want to know me, given she hasn't so far, but I want to meet her for myself, even if she doesn't know it's me. Like, I thought I might pretend to have the wrong address or something. Knock on her door and ask where something is. So if you could let me know where she is. If you have the details."

"It's in the address book, son. It's always been there. In the cupboard in the dining room. It's under 'I'."

"What's her name now? Her married name?"

"Mo Sampson."

"Then why is she listed under 'I'?"

"Because she's an idiot, son, for not having wanted you." He sighed. "You know where I am if you need me. If you want me to go see her with you."

"I think Dela might come with me."

"Sounds like a good idea. Seeing another woman might make her less defensive. Come on now, times getting on and us Andersons are busy boys."

I moved swiftly over to my dad and gave him a hug.

"Thanks, Pops. You're the best."

"Dunno about that but I try my best," he said. "And that's all you can do."

Dela was already waiting when I arrived. She was seated in the boulevard, wrapped in a massive white puffa coat. She looked like an igloo.

She got up and approached me. Her gloved hands were wrapped around a travel cup filled with coffee. Its scent wafted through the cool air.

"You said eight and it's ten past," she scolded.

"Sorry. At the last minute I decided to ask my dad about my mum."

"Oooh, and what did he say?"

"That her address is in our address book and also, he's glad you agreed to come with me."

"All we need to do then is sort out when you want to go."

"Yeah, I need to think about it. Now, can you just give me a minute to talk to the vamps about what today's agenda is and about your plans."

"Sure."

I walked into the half-standing building and approached the tall, thin man with purple hair who was directing the vamp builders.

"Morning, Zane."

"Hey there, Nick. We don't need much from you this morning. We'll be ready to sort first fixes soon."

"I've brought Callie's sister around. She'll advise us on what her sister would want. Mya's busy today."

"Thank f—" He stopped himself. "What a shame." He looked over at Dela. "Please tell me she's not going to be too demanding."

"Dela's great. Also, I've drawn up those sketches for her new home. You able to take a look?"

"Oh, this is the woman whose house we're building next. Good to know." He looked her over again. "Fae, right?"

I nodded.

"I can work on these this morning, no problem. I'll do it while you talk to Jack and Oscar about what they need knocking down."

"Thanks, Zane."

He nodded and walked away. I spoke to the guys and then went back out to Dela.

"Hey, can I bother you to grab me a latte from *Saverstore*? Mitzi's put a machine in temporarily apparently."

"Huh, didn't take her long to jump in my sister's grave. If I go there and she's selling cupcakes there'll be trouble."

I began to regret asking but I was thirsty. "Can you get me a *Double Decker* too, and a large bottle of *Orange Tango*?"

"I thought I was here to design a home and store?"

"You will be. There's just a little more demolition to do first."

"Fine."

I went in my pocket to get some money, but she waved me off.

"Forget it. I can shout you a drink and a chocolate bar. Just hurry up so the store can be rebuilt and I can be inside again. It's bloody freezing out here."

I looked down at myself, dressed only in a t-shirt.

My ancestry and job meant I was not only used to working outside, but I rarely felt the cold.

"You're not normal," she huffed.

"I'm hot stuff," I yelled at her retreating back.

"You and her got something going on?" Zane asked, standing by my side as Dela went out of sight.

"She won't date anyone from Gnarly," I told him. "It's her rule."

"Rules are made to be broken, my friend." He slapped me on the back. "Now, come on, there are other things need knocking down before you start on her walls."

CHAPTER

TEN

Dela

I'd woken up in a surprisingly good mood. Maybe it was because all my belongings had stayed put and I'd not been crushed to death by a personal effects avalanche during the night. In actual fact, I realised it was because deep down I'd been worried about what Mya was doing to my sister's business. Now I could oversee things, I could make sure it would be the place of her dreams. I would make some changes though. My sister loved pink. Like loved it probably as much as she loved her new husband. Not everyone felt the same though and the cupcake café having been a 'pink paradise' to Callie, had given customers a headache at times. Regulars got used to it. Other patrons forgave the colour scheme the moment a cupcake reached their tastebuds. But now the place could appeal to most.

I reached Gnarly's convenience store and pushed open the door. Mitzi was whistling to herself. She looked at me with her small, dark eyes and stopped.

"Morning, Dela. Don't usually see you this early in a morning. I'd presume you were doing a walk of shame, but you're dressed appropriately for the day."

"I've come to get Nick a coffee and apparently you have a brand-new machine in-situ..."

"Gnarly needs its coffee and the café is currently out of action. Anyway, look at it." She pointed to the machine. "It's so...shiny." I watched as Mitzi almost preened. She stretched her shoulders and then ran a hand knocking her white fringe out of her face. The rest of her hair, long and jet-black stayed perfectly still. Mitzi liked her hair products.

"The café will be up and running again by Thursday latest," I informed her.

"Keep your hair on, Delphinium. People need coffee and I actually sold it first, albeit in jars. You know, being the first building to open up in Gnarly, my ancestors pretty much had everything first."

I threw a *Double Decker* onto the counter and went off in search of the large bottles of orange pop.

Seeing a packet of chocolate chip cookies that I figured would dunk nicely in my own drink, I picked them up, followed by the bottle of pop and added those to the counter. "Can I pay for these and for two lattes please?"

She took my money and then handed me two cardboard cups. "Instructions are on the machine." While I went over, she stared at the fifty pence piece I'd handed her along with the rest of the money. Magpie shifters. Anything shiny and they were completely distracted. She didn't even look up as I left.

After handing Nick his coffee which he drank straight down—inside his mouth must have a heat protection coating or some such witchcraft—I held back and watched as he knocked down walls until a vampire distracted me with house plans. Having asked me inside a small portacabin, I saw a table was covered with large sheets of paper.

Zane had taken what Nick had sketched—and Nick's sketches had been fantastic—but now they were elaborate, intricately drawn plans showing a family home that unbelievably, due to their work speed, could be erected as a real-life dwelling by the end of the week.

"This is just incredible. It's mind-blowing to think this will be standing there in the woods in days if the plans go through."

"They'll go through," Zane said. "There's nothing else to be done with that piece of land, it may as well be the location for someone's dream house."

I nodded, but I felt a strain as my lips formed a smile. It was my dream house all right. Designed for my future dreams. While it was beautiful, I couldn't help but feel that until I found my Mr Right the place would feel a little empty.

When Nick was done with his demolition, he took the plans from Zane and left to take them down to the community centre ready for tomorrow evening's council meeting. I followed Zane back into the portacabin where he took me through the ideas Mya had given him for the store. The half-pink, half-black idea.

"Dear God, no." I looked at some vision boards and mocked-up illustrations. "It looks like a Fruit Salad chew and a Black Jack one had a baby. It's awful."

"That's what I thought, but Mya was pretty

insistent, with the whole pink cupcake/black book-store theme."

"My sister loves pink, as you'll well know because you've seen it demolished, but this is going to be a space where she'll be working alongside her husband and the bookstore staff. Also, it's time to put the customers first, so I'm thinking very pale pink walls. Framed photos of buns and cups of coffee, or slices of cake alongside teapots, both alongside books. You get what I mean?"

Zane nodded. "We could start with purchased photos and then once the café is opened you could replace them with genuine photos from the shop."

"Good thinking."

Zane moved to his chair and held his fingertip against a button so the screen came to life. He clicked on a few things and the café interior came on the screen. "Pull up a seat and let's get this changed."

We worked for a good hour, but by the time we were finished there was a café come bookstore that would hopefully make everyone happy, with an area for patrons only interested in the food and drink, morphing over into comfy sofas and larger tables where books could be placed.

"I'm meeting a guy called Merrin shortly," Zane

explained. "He's going to make the countertops and shelving from reclaimed wood."

"Oh he'll do a fantastic job I'm sure," I reassured him. "Although if you like I can hang around and work with the both of you to make sure it keeps with what we think will work. Merrin can sometimes go a bit rogue if he gets an idea in his head. It's the artist in him."

"If you don't mind staying around, I'd appreciate it," Zane said, and I noted he had a lovely smile. Unfortunately, I then noted he was wearing a wedding ring. The guy had been wafting his hands around showing me plans all morning, you'd think I'd have spotted that earlier. I was pleased my mind wards were up so Zane couldn't hear my thoughts.

I was stunned when I walked back outside to see that the bottom half of the building was finished. Vamp speed was something else. Walls were almost plastered, and Zane informed me that the plaster was enchanted to dry quickly. "The lower part of this building, the shop, will be finished completely by tomorrow latest, other than whatever Merrin does with the bookstore part. Now, I'd just worked on extending what was already there for the apartment above, but seeing as we have time while we wait for

Merrin to arrive, do you want to go through those plans with me too?" Zane asked.

"Absolutely I do," I told him, a genuine smile coming over my face. I was enjoying designing this space, far more so than I'd enjoyed designing my house, which was disconcerting. I put it down to the fact that the café would not only benefit my sister but also Gnarly in general.

Zane said the kitchen part of the building was handled as he'd consulted with a London based café owner and basically copied the design. As he showed me the plans for the upper level, I couldn't believe this was replacing the place where I'd lived. The floorspace was now doubled.

"So I thought floor-to-ceiling windows that looked out over the boulevard. Same concept as your place, that you can see out, but people can't see in. Large, open-plan living room. With your sister being fae I thought natural woods, cream walls, green accessories. Maybe some potted ferns, things like that?"

"Oh yes, that would be amazing. Bring the outside in. Chocolate-brown, thick pile carpet in the bedroom, like earthy tones; reclaimed wood shelving, and a mirror done the same way. Merrin will sort that I'm sure. In fact, he probably already has them in his warehouse."

The day had flown and before I knew it, Merrin had arrived and joined us.

Merrin was slim and wan. Tall with long, dark straggly hair, his cheeks were sunken and he had dark circles under his eyes. He was also a zombie. Yup, Merrin had died at some point and been re-animated, but he didn't chase people and try to eat their flesh. He was still who he was before he died, just thinner and paler.

He also lived more in his head than in the real world and would stare at his sculptures and other creative work for ages, making you wonder at times if he'd passed away again.

Zane directed us into the part of the store that was to be the bookshop after showing Merrin the illustrations.

"This is no problem. With the measurements I can make all the shelving and the counters. I already have a suitable mirror and also, I have picture frames that will match, ensuring that the café side of things kind of meanders into the bookstore. He made his fingers wave as if showing a trickling stream. Also, the tables. I have suitable tables and some wooden chairs. You'll just need to organise the couches. The sisters will have those." He turned to me and his elongated, thin fingers tapped on his chin. "No pink walls. No, no, no. Reclaimed wood will not suit pink. Cream. Yes, cream. Leave the pink to the cupcakes in the pictures and maybe the accessories, yes? She already has those: the plates, the cups, the cutlery. He moved around the space, eerily walking in a way where he hardly picked up his feet, so he seemed to glide across the floor. "The vampires don't care what a place looks like. They've seen so many things. As long as they have interest, and a refrigerator full of blood, they will be happy. Put a small fridge under the counter or a packet of those emergency tablets they use in the till. Better to be careful so that they don't drain the customers."

Zane and I exchanged a look, but Merrin was lost, staring at the walls. After a few moments, I called his name.

"Merrin? Can I get you a drink or anything? The store has a hot drinks machine I can go to."

"No, thank you, Dela. I shall go now and gather everything needed into my van. I will be back tomorrow morning when you shall arrange for Aria to be here so we may work together and get the bookstore completed."

Again I looked at Zane.

"I will negotiate with Aria," Zane said. "Thank you for your time, Merrin. You have improved upon our plans, and we very much look forward to working with you tomorrow."

"She won't like it," Merrin said.

"Pardon?"

"She won't like it," Merrin repeated.

A chill swept over my body. Merrin sometimes came out with strange 'knowings' or predictions. Not very often, but when he did, he was always right and so we took heed.

"Do you mean my sister? Will she not like what we've done?"

My face must have shown my terror because Zane's expression mirrored what I was feeling. His mouth was open and brow creased.

"The other vampire woman who will work here. She will annoy me, thinking she knows better."

"No other vampire woman is working here, other than Aria," I said.

"We'll see," Merrin told me, and with that he wiggled his fingers in goodbye and left the building.

"What a strange man," Zane said.

"Indeed. His work is beautiful though."

Zane nodded. "I shall take your word for it. Will you be able to be around tomorrow in case this other female vampire appears? Do you think he meant Mya?"

"Oh God, I bet he does. She can't work here alongside Aria. They'll kill each other. I bet that's it. Even though Mya has enough to do with the wayward, I bet she'll not be able to stand the thought of Aria hanging around with Callie so much. She might panic that she'll lose her new best friend, especially as Aria is Lawrie's best friend's wife."

Zane ran a hand through his hair. "Please tell me you're able to be here tomorrow too."

I nodded. "I don't think I have a choice, Zane. Because if the two of them fought in here, there'd be no business still standing."

CHAPTER ELEVEN

Nick

With the plans safely dropped off at the community centre and logged by the secretary as received, I now had the rest of the day to myself. I decided I'd go home and help my dad in the workshop.

Pushing open the door, I found, as expected, my father looking frazzled, as he walked the lines, inspecting the elves' work. As I approached him, I noted the droplets of sweat beaded on his brow. He wiped the back of his hand across his forehead and gave me a half-smile. "Son, this is a pleasant surprise. What are you doing here?"

"I got finished early at the site, so I thought I'd come help out."

"Oh that's okay. He already has an assistant

today, don't you, Stan-the-man?" Mya emerged from behind a storage unit.

Suddenly the frazzled expression on Dad's face became clearer.

"Mya, what are you doing here?"

"It's my covert mission I was talking to you about this morning." She tapped the side of her nose again. "I can't tell you or I'd have to kill you."

My eyes widened.

"Joking, I'm joking. No one is going to die today. No one at all. Nope, not on my watch. Hey, elf. Look up," she yelled before flying over and lifting their face up and staring into their eyes. "False alarm. As you were," she said, coming back to my father's side.

"How long have you been here, Mya?"

"Since I saw you this morning."

My dad exhaled audibly through his nose.

"And how long will you be here for?"

"Hopefully not long, but I have to stay until my mission is complete. You could say I'm saving Christmas. That's it. Operation Saving Christmas."

She went up to the elf again. "Are you in there?" The elf emitted a shriek, that had Mya step back in alarm, a hand over her ears.

"That has to be demonic, right?" she asked us.

"No, that's a really pissed off elf that's telling you

to back off or it's going to bite off your nose," my dad explained.

"Oh. Sorry," she told the elf, who threw down his hammer and stalked off.

"I'll be back when she's gone," he shouted.

"Mya." My dad beckoned her over. "Do you have to do your covert mission here? Are you positive? Because if you make any more of my elves down tools, you won't have saved Christmas, you'll have ruined it."

"Dad, you go and talk to Spike, and I'll have a chat with Mya here. See if we can't find a solution."

"Sounds like a plan." Dad wandered off and Mya moved to set off after him.

"Mya!" I snapped.

She tapped her foot against the floor. "I have to be with him at all times."

"Come with me. I have a way you can be with him without actually being with him." I took her through to our security room where I dismissed the elf watching the screens. Dad came on screen in the dining room area.

"There you go. You can watch over the whole building and whizz in if necessary. Now why do you have to watch my dad, and do not tell me it's a secret you can't reveal. If my dad's in danger I want to know and I want to help. I'll join your covert mission. Just give me any paperwork I need to sign."

Mya rubbed the back of her neck and started manically pacing. "I'm not supposed to tell anyone. When I told Callie she was going to die, it was a trap set by Death and he was not very happy with me. I ended up causing her to almost die because I said it in the first place."

"He's going to die?" I shrieked.

"What? I didn't say that." Mya was now visibly sweating, which I didn't think I'd ever seen a cold skinned vampire do before. She had a pained expression and started picking the skin around her pinkie finger.

"*Mya!* Is my dad going to die?"

"I'm not allowed to say. I absolutely promised I'd never tell anyone anything from The Book of the Dead ever again."

"Mya, how about if you sing me a song? Hmmm?" I suggested.

"Why? I'm not feeling very jolly today and I don't have a very good voice. There's no wonder you have trouble getting a date with Dela if you make strange requests like this when I'm in the middle of sorting out a potentially dangerous situation."

"It's not about the voice, it's about the *lyrics.*" I

hoped to God the penny dropped soon because my insides were churning.

"Ohhhhhhh. Right." She cleared her throat and then started singing Yello's '*Oh Yeah*'.

And my churning stomach changed to me full blown retching.

"Ow! Did you just fucking bite me?" I stared at my wrist where two beads of blood appeared. Mya grabbed my wrist again and licked across. I started to feel like I'd been given a slight sedative. "You lied. It's not Dad who's going to die, is it? It's me. You're going to murder me." I fell into the chair, feeling spaced. "And I'm going to be powerless to resist."

"I've bit you, so you calm the fuck down," Mya said. "You said you wanted to help me if your dad was in danger, but you can't very well do that if you're trying not to be sick in the corner."

While I processed the feeling of calm floating through my body, Mya sat down on the chair next to me and explained about the escaped wayward.

"So I need to find them and fast, because otherwise there's not going to be a merry Christmas for anyone, least of all your father."

"And the book doesn't tell you how he dies?"

"Who said anything about him dying? I have not said a word of such a thing. I've not broken any rules or things I agreed to. Haven't we had a good sing-song though? Forgot how much I liked that song," Mya wittered on.

I put my head in my hands. "My dad can't die. Not just because he's Father Christmas but because he's my dad."

"I know." Suddenly Mya wasn't as chipper and full on as she had been. "That's why I'm here. We're pretty sure this is an error caused by the escaped wayward and that your father's not meant to pop off. Not yet anyway."

I ran my hands down my face and exhaled through my fingers. "But it's a reminder that one day he will. Even though we live for many years, one day we die, he'll die."

"I already died. It's not so bad." She shrugged. "You don't know what comes after for you. It could be good, but in the meantime, live life to the full, Nick." She turned and her stare became more intense. "And that means if you think Dela is the one for you then give it your best shot... but if she decides you are not the one for her, move on."

Mya was talking sense. Had I landed on an alternate universe?

"You're right. No sense flogging a dead horse. I'd already decided that I'd try to get to know her while I help with her house and then I'd give up if I'd not won her over by then. What you've said has helped me to confirm that. You can't make someone love you."

"I probably can because I'm a badass vampire with a touch of death that means my power of suggestion abilities are off the charts, but I'm not going to because Death will remove my Big D privileges and that is a fate worse than death."

Okay, the sense hadn't lasted for long, mad Mya was back.

"So, we spend the afternoon looking for an escaped demon spirit?"

"Or good spirit. The jury is still out until I review his case."

"Well, I have no idea how we do this, but you watch via the cameras and I'll watch from the shop floor seeing as I'm helping for the rest of the day."

"Cool. Do you by any chance have any cushions or a throw, so I can get comfy? This chair is a bit basic."

"Are you used to a throne now, my queen?" I raised a brow.

"No, I just have a really bony arse that this wooden chair isn't doing any favours for and being a vampire I run really cold."

"Hey, Dad, I've got Mya safely tucked away in the security room, so what can I help with?"

"If you can go to the staff room and see if you can coax back the three elves she drove away while accusing them of being demonic that would help. So many of the elves have been acting weird today. It's holding up production of the life-size Edward from Twilight cardboard cut-outs and they are in huge demand this year."

An elf walked past and whispered something to my dad and then he clutched his ear.

My dad's eyes flashed red as the scared elf ran off also clutching his ear.

"She liked the other one, the bitch," my father said, sounding like he had a sore throat.

"Pardon?"

My dad's eyes had returned to normal, to the point where I wondered if I'd been seeing things. Then the next thing I knew, I felt a popping sensation through my ear and suddenly I was no longer in charge of my own body.

"Nick?" My dad's eyes were wide as he looked at me.

"Fuck the elves. Are you making cut-outs of the other Twilight characters too, so that people like my fucking ex can say 'Oh, if only you were more like... like...'" I clicked my fingers while the demon thought.

"Jacob?" My father asked.

"No," I heard myself snarl. "Not *my* wife. She always had to be fucking *different*. Jasper. That's the one she liked. Fucking Jasper."

"I'm not making cut-outs of Jasper," my father said. The next thing I knew Mya was in my face.

"Get out, demon," she ordered while shaking out her right hand. "Oh no. Why isn't the sphere appearing? I must have bloody performance anxiety."

My legs moved and I found myself running outside, looking this way and that until I spotted a cat on the top of a wall. With speed I'd never possessed before, I ran over to the wall and the pop sounded in my ear as the demon exited. The cat's eyes flashed red before it jumped over the other side of the wall and ran away.

Mya came running up to me. "Wayne, stop this. You cannot escape your fate." She barrelled into me, knocking me to the floor, where she sat atop my thighs, and held down my shoulders.

Her hair fell into my face as she leaned over me, her eyes laser focused on mine. "You will submit to me," she ordered, and I felt my own free will disappearing for the second time in almost as many minutes.

"I am yours to command," I said.

"Wayne, you will leave Nick's body and come into this sphere." A red and gold sphere hovered above her hand.

"I am not Wayne, I am Nick," I said.

"Huh?" Mya replied.

"Wayne has left the building, sweetheart," I heard Death say as he walked over from the shadows. "Last seen inhabiting a cat."

Mya smirked.

"Do not say it, Mya," he warned.

"Say what?" she asked Death.

"Whatever you were going to say connected with the word 'pussy'."

"You're such a spoilsport."

"Are you going to give Nick his voice back anytime soon so he can plead with you to get off him?" Death folded his arms over his chest.

Mya then realised the position she was in. "Oh, erm, yes, of course. Sorry there, Nick." She crawled off me.

"I apologise for my significant other," Death said. "I understand she has been turning up to see you in your bedroom in a morning and has now launched herself upon your body. I am sure there is a logical explanation for all of this behaviour isn't there, Mya, other than Nick being extremely buff?"

"Every bit of it is connected with either the wedding present or the escapee," she said. Then she whispered to me, "But if I was single, I'd deffo try my luck, because fuck me you're huge."

"Can you kill me? Right here, right now?" I asked Death.

"No one is going to die at the present moment," Death replied, looking at his app.

"I saved him?" Mya shrieked. "You know, the person who I told no one was in danger. No one at all."

He raised a brow at her. "It appears that our escapee is causing a gremlin as it were with The Book and the app. It went from predicting Santa's death, to Nick's, and now while it's in the cat it's fine because of course, cats have nine lives. We just have to keep our eyes and ears open around Gnarly and around the Book and the app until Wayne is captured. I trust you will keep this to yourself, Nick, but come to us should you see any further evidence of Wayne."

"Of course. We don't want widespread panic in the village."

"Indeed."

"Okay, I need to get back to the house," Mya said. "I have to dispatch the wayward there while I have the chance."

Just like that, Mya disappeared, shortly followed afterwards by Death. Then my dad appeared.

"You okay, son?"

"Yeah, I'm fine. You?"

"Yeah, only I wasn't taking any chances standing near to Grim like you did. Once I heard he wasn't here for you, I kept myself back."

I chuckled, and then Dad laughed, and then hysteria came over us both while we processed the bizarreness of what had just happened. I knew one thing though. I needed to talk to a witch about a protection spell to stop a demon being able to take over my body as soon as I could.

CHAPTER TWELVE

Dela

After returning to my very cramped room at the twins' place, I soon realised that the sooner my own house was built, the better, and in the meantime, I needed to find myself a man. I clicked into my dating app and had a look at new matches.

None of them were for me. I felt like Goldilocks as I looked through, saying that one's too small, (in height, you filthy animal). Unfortunately, there were none that were just right.

While the twins were still at work, I decided to avail myself of the bathroom and had a long, luxurious soak in the tub followed by a pamper session. Feeling chilled out, I started preparing that evening's dinner, and then I gave the place a general tidy round, even getting out the vacuum cleaner.

I sank down on the sofa while I waited for the twins to come home so I could start the dinner. What was wrong with me? I was so unsettled. It had to be all these potential changes in my life. Without further ado, I went into my bedroom and unearthed my belongings until I found a small jewellery box where between a layer of cloth and the base I had Sheridan's number on a piece of paper.

There was no time like the present.

"Hello, Sheridan Rose speaking."

"Hello, Sheridan. My name is Delphinium and I..."

"Have a sister called Calendula and live in Gnarly Fell?"

"You remember us?"

Her warm voice let out a soft chuckle. "It was only five years ago, Dela. Not five hundred."

"True."

"What can I do for you, Dela? Is everything still okay in Gnarly?"

"Yes, fine. We love it here. Callie has just got married actually... to a vampire."

I thought she might sound shocked, but all Sheridan said was, "How lovely, give her my best."

"The reason I'm calling is that I want to know more about my family and where I come from. Callie knows that I intended to get in touch with you about it.”

“And how does she feel about that?”

“She has mixed feelings,” I said, erring on the side of tact and caution.

“If it’s okay with you, Dela, I’d like to come and see you face-to-face in Gnarly first. We can have a good chat then at what’s brought this on and the potential repercussions of this.”

“You won’t change my mind.”

“I don’t want to change your mind. I do however want to make sure you’re okay and find out what has preceded this decision, because I’m picking up some kind of urgency or restlessness in your tone. I’m wondering if this is a reaction to Callie getting married and her moving on?”

I sighed. “What time tomorrow?”

After cooking and eating dinner, I still felt restless and lost. The twins were chatting about their day and I hoped I was nodding in all the right places. When my phone rang and I saw it was Nick, I dived to answer it quickly, hoping he wanted to go view the house plot again or something so I could get out.

"Hey," I answered.

"Dela?"

"Who else would it be?" I laughed.

"I'm just checking in case someone else picked up your phone. Want to make sure I'm talking to the right person before I explain my completely batshit day."

"It's me, so what can I do for you?"

"Your friend. The one we met at the restaurant. She's a witch, right?"

"Chantelle. Yes. But she gets her spells mixed up a lot."

"Oh. Well can you ask her if she knows a witch who can do an enchantment on me so that my body cannot be possessed by an evil spirit?"

"What the heck happened to you today?"

"Something I really could have done without."

I knew I could have got him to explain all this on the phone, but I desperately wanted to get out. "Want to meet at the bistro and tell me all about it? I've spoken to my fae contact today about getting in touch with my family. We could exchange stories and advice. That's if your dad doesn't need you to help this evening."

"My dad's told me to take the evening off after

today, so that sounds perfect. I could use a couple of pints of beer to be honest."

"Okay. Meet you there at eight?"

"It's a non-date," he said.

Nick was already inside when I arrived and was chatting to Chantelle at the bar. I felt my body tense as I watched her interactions with him. Nick had his back to me at that moment, so I couldn't see his features, but Chantelle was clearly flirting with him. Her eye contact was firm and intense, like there was no one in the bar but the two of them, and she was leaning forward to listen, which I guessed would give Nick a clear shot of her tits down her top. Her fingers brushed against her own throat as a smile lit across her features, and I was over there interrupting before I could check myself over my behaviour.

"Hey, Del." Chantelle greeted me with such a genuine and large smile that I felt guilty at the fact that just seconds before I'd wanted to break up her chat with Nick. What kind of friend was I? I wouldn't date him so there was no reason why Chantelle couldn't flirt with him. Nick had also spun around on his seat to greet me.

"Chantelle has agreed to get in touch with her mentor about sorting out my protection spell."

"Hopefully Alicia will let me perform it under her mentorship," Chantelle said at a rapid pace, excitement in her tone. "She's very pleased with my progress this week. I only made one mistake, and she was quickly able to bring Medina back from the dead."

Nick went so pale he was almost translucent. I looked at his half-drunk pint. "Same again, Nick?"

"Yes please and a double whisky. I'll get them," he insisted.

The bleeper Nick had been given to wait for a table went off then. "You go get seated and one of the staff will bring your drinks over," Chantelle instructed, and so Nick hopped off his bar stool and we made our way to a member of wait staff who showed us to our table.

"You have no idea how much I needed a friend and a pint," Nick said. "Jason is out on a date tonight so I thought I was going to be on my own for the night, ruminating about being possessed."

"I thought I was going to be in the twins' house listening to those two trying to hold separate conversations all night. I love them both, but they've always been strange and right now they're acting even weirder. My bedroom is now full to bursting with my belongings so it's not the most relaxing place to escape to at present either. So, spill, what happened this afternoon?"

"I'm not supposed to say really." He chewed on his bottom lip.

"Are we not kind of besties, confiding in each other about all our deepest secrets?" I shrugged, trying not to show how desperate I was to find out all the goss.

"Besties?" His upper lip ticked as it tried to resist amusement, but then he broke into a guffaw.

"Okay, confidantes," I huffed. "Just spill already!"

So he did. He told me about the escaped spirit and how it had jumped from his father, to him, to the cat that finally escaped.

"Oh, that's what I saw." I sighed in relief.

"What?" He paused to examine my face.

"When I was waiting at yours the other night. Your dad's eyes flashed red, and well, I kinda thought that although I now knew he was Santa, that he also might have been... Satan."

That was it. Nick laughed so loud it made his previous guffaw seem like a whisper. The guy was not small and his gruff laughter echoed around the place so that everyone turned towards us. All I could think though was that I'd given him a giggle on a day where it seemed like he most needed one. It made me feel good to see the laughter dance across his features, making his eyes sparkle with both merriment and a dash of water from tears of mirth building, and a flush to his cheeks.

He looked so damn attractive that I realised I wanted to jump his bones there and then.

"No," I shouted out loud.

Nick stopped laughing abruptly. "What?"

"Oh, erm sorry, I just was thinking out loud about the fact I'd considered buying some cheese and onion crisps, but I've realised salt and vinegar would go a lot better with red wine."

"Stop trying to change the subject and let me laugh about the fact you thought my kind and caring father, who spends his whole year focusing on people's happiness, was not only an evil entity, but *the* evil entity, the ruler of Hell."

"His eyes flashed red and he said some evil things," I protested, but my words fell on deaf ears as Nick started laughing again. Finally, he managed to control himself.

"Oh, Dela, I'm so glad we met tonight. This was exactly what I needed. A bloody good laugh."

It was then I noticed that there was more than one set of female eyes on us. Some were looking over, their gaze fixed on the handsome man who'd just been laughing his head off; and others fixed me with a glare of sheer envy before quickly looking away. I noticed that Chantelle was one of the ones whose expression was a little envious.

"Okay, so getting back to your possession... do you feel okay now? I'm guessing you're not, given you want a spell of protection. I completely get that, because you lost control over yourself which must have been pretty scary."

"It really was. Mainly because I was still there, still in my body but squashed down, while the entity did what he wanted. I could feel his thoughts. He was full of jealousy about his ex-wife and wanted to escape his fate from the Home of Wayward Souls."

"So Mya is on a mission to re-capture him?"

"Yes. I said I'd keep a look out for the cat or any strange behaviour from residents as the guy jumped easily from us all with just a pop in our ears."

"He could be out of Gnarly by now. You know how cats get around."

Nick shook his head. "No, apparently he is tied to Gnarly itself. His fate gets resolved here and it's just a matter of time. Unfortunately, he can put people's lives at risk while possessing them because he has no care given he's already dead. If he kills one of us he can just jump to another." Nick went on to explain how his father and then he had for a moment been fated to die.

The thought of Nick dying was too much on top of my awareness of the women in the bar's lustful gazes and the effect of all the red wine I'd consumed at a rapid rate.

I was out of my seat and I launched myself at him, sitting across his lap and fixing my mouth on his. His mouth replied to mine hungrily, our tongues tangling together until I realised what the fuck I was doing.

I. WAS. KISSING. NICK.

I broke away and jumped back to my seat.

"Oh my god, it took me over," I lied, feeling at my ears in order to fake the entity having popped in and out.

Nick looked at me strangely.

"I felt it. It must be stopped." I had felt *it*, if *it* had been Nick's dick that I'd kind of been squirming on, and not the evil entity.

"You were possessed just then, when you threw yourself on my lap and kissed me like your life depended on it?" Nick double-checked.

"Yes! I felt the pop in my ear and then I didn't know what I was doing."

"And the guy with a grudge against his ex-wife decided he fancied a snog with a six foot two, tattooed builder? Hmmm."

I was sure I was visibly sweating. I pulled at my top while inside I cringed and prayed he stopped discussing my recent action and accepted my explanation of possession. "I got the impression he wanted to try out everything while he could, and then just like that he was gone again. I am so sorry." I held up my hands in a 'What can you do?' gesture.

"Well, I'm not. The spirit is a damn good kisser," Nick said. "Anyway, why don't you tell me about your day."

Grateful he'd given me an out, despite the fact we clearly both knew I hadn't been possessed, I told him about my chat with Sheridan.

CHAPTER THIRTEEN

Nick

It was very difficult to try to act normal when the object of your affections had just launched herself at you, straddled your lap, (resulting in a huge hard-on), and then leapt off claiming to have been possessed.

The only thing Dela had just been possessed by was lust, but she'd clearly regretted her impulsivity and was now back-tracking. Being the gentleman I was, I would let her, although she surely knew I didn't believe the entity had just popped in for a swift ear cleaning session with my companion. No one had been remotely near us when it had happened and the only thing red was Dela's wine.

Now as I listened to Dela tell me about her call to Sheridan, I was only half-listening as I tried my best to control my facial expression into one of understanding and compassion around her meeting the fae woman tomorrow, when all I wanted to do was jump around the bistro, punch the air, and do a sing-song based around the words, 'Ha, you want me'. Her resistance towards dating me even though she found me attractive, was clearly being stretched to its limits, which meant I was getting somewhere in spending time with her and wearing down those stubborn defences of hers.

"So basically she wouldn't tell me anything until she's sure of my motivation for wanting to know." Dela sighed.

"It's understandable. Something as important as this shouldn't be discussed by phone. It is better in person. That way she's on hand to support you if she has to tell you anything distressing."

Dela's eyes widened. "Do you think that's why? Maybe my fae parents are dead?"

"I don't know. No-one except Sheridan knows anything, so don't start assuming things. Just wait until she comes to see you tomorrow and then you'll have all the information you seek."

"Yeah, I guess."

"So did you decide on salt and vinegar crisps because you've not ordered any?" I teased.

"Oh, erm."

"I'm going to order some nachos. Want to share?"

"Yes please. I need to soak up some of this wine. I feel a little woozy and I can't be dealing with a hangover tomorrow."

I beckoned over the waitress. "Can we have a large nachos to share, a pint of beer for me, a latte for my friend, and a carafe of water for the table?"

"Of course." The waitress left us to organise our order.

"Are you back at the build tomorrow?" Dela asked me.

"No. My part is done. The vamps will be finished with the building by tomorrow morning. Thursday morning they'll hopefully be starting on yours."

"That seems so strange to me. That by the end of the week I could have my own place in the woods."

I noticed that her posture sagged a little.

"What is it, Dela? What's wrong? If it's moving too fast, we can get the permissions through, but delay building."

She ran a hand through her hair. "I'm fine. I'm going to blame how fast I've drunk this wine. My head feels like chaos."

"Or it might be the evil entity?"

"What evi— oh yes, the man has messed with my brain as he passed through." She placed her hands on her chest and took a deep inhale. "I can't help thinking that I'll have a house for a family in the woods when I'm a single woman who likes to be in the heart of the action. I'm building a house for future me, and that's not who I am right now. I'm feeling more than a bit confused right now," she confessed.

"Dela, you have options." I sought to re-assure her. "You can decide to not build it at the moment, or at all even. You could build it and rent it to someone else and have it as an investment. Or you can move in and have a roommate so you're not on your own. Building isn't starting until Thursday morning at the earliest and I'm part of that team, so you have a full twenty-four hours to think about it. Unless, of course, you decide to change the scope of the building, in which case we'd need to be submitting new plans. In that case I'd suggest withdrawing your current ones and re-submitting next month to give yourself some thinking space. You do have a lot happening in your life at the moment."

"You must think I'm a complete idiot," she said, looking down at her feet.

"Only in that you continue to deny your major

attraction to me," I teased, having gained confidence from my continued alcohol intake. It was good the waitress took that moment to deliver the drinks and nachos as my companion had looked flustered and very un-Dela like as she'd looked up at me with wide eyes.

"Talking of tasty things." I stuck my hand in the dish and brought out a nacho covered in melted cheese and salsa. "Tuck in."

While we ate, Dela asked me if I'd thought any more about contacting my mother.

"I want to, but I keep going over in my mind about the best way to do it."

"Well I can come with you tomorrow if you like," she said.

"Aren't you busy enough tomorrow?" I checked with her. "You're overseeing the décor on the café, meeting Sheridan, need to think about your potential new home, and now you want to visit my mother?"

"Look, I'm a nosy bitch and I want to see what she's like, and you need to see what she's like, so come on, let's do this. Anyhow, I'll be able to update you about how my visit from Sheridan went. I'm sure I'll be needing my bestie's advice. Of course, that's if you survive Chantelle's spell."

"Don't." I shivered. "I'm starting to wonder if

possession by an evil spirit is preferable to the tinkering of a trainee witch."

We finished eating and drinking and said our goodbyes. Dela was stubborn about making her own way home and I let her get on with it. After all, out of the two of us, I was the one who'd been rendered the most helpless today, not her.

When I got back to the house, I popped into the workshop to see my father. He looked in good spirits and it was nice to see him looking relaxed and chipper for a change.

"You're looking a lot better."

"I am, son. I am. Because I had a fantastic idea and I have you to thank."

"You do?"

"You got me thinking when you talked about Fen. Woman busied herself with consoling all the broken-hearted of Gnarly and of course now the curse is lifted she doesn't have that to do so much. I headed down the boulevard to grab a few bits from the minimarket earlier this evening and I saw her strolling around looking in the shop windows. At first, I thought she was Christmas shopping, so I asked if she needed any help, but after chatting to her I realised the woman was bored. I asked her if she fancied taking on a supervisory role here at the workshop while it was so busy. She's starting in the morning. Also, now Mya's not around the elves are all back to full strength. So all is well at present, son. All is very well."

And it was at that moment I realised that my father had a crush on Fenella and that I wasn't the only one suffering from a case of unrequited love.

"How was your evening, lad, anyway? Where did you get to?"

"I met Dela at the bistro to catch up on a few things."

"Judging by your expression, I'm guessing there's no progress happening there still?"

I decided to be honest with my dad in the hope that at some point in the near future I could talk to him about opening up about his own feelings for Fenella. I wondered how long he'd been harbouring feelings for my best friend's mother.

"It's crazy, Dad. She won't date me because I'm from Gnarly and she will only date outside of the fell for in case things don't work out, because it would be 'awkward'. Yet tonight she kissed me. She kissed me and then told me the entity had possessed her."

"And you're sure it hadn't?"

"Positive. But it is what it is. I'm giving it until the new year and then I'm moving on. We're currently doing this supportive friends thing and we're around each other because of the building work. But new year, new focus as regards my love life, Dad. The curse has been lifted and we have a chance at happiness."

"Aye, lad, we do," he said, looking into the distance for a moment, before turning back around to me. "But for now, keep Dela at the top of your Christmas wish list because you never know what Santa can do."

"Dad, please don't interfere."

He tapped the side of his nose. "Believe in Christmas miracles, son." With that he made his excuses and returned to work.

The following morning, I had a text from Chantelle. We had exchanged numbers at the bar.

Chantelle: One pm at Alicia's house, 7 Tree Root Walk.

Nick: I'll be there, thank you.

Chantelle: See you then.

I felt nervous after what Dela had told me about Chantelle's ability to mess up spells on a regular basis. Then I thought about learning to drive. You could in effect wipe out a road user were it not for the instructor sitting beside you and that's how I needed to look at it. Chantelle was the 'learner driver' and this Alicia woman was her instructor. I was sure all would be fine.

After getting ready, I took the stairs two at a time to get to my morning hot drink faster but paused when I heard laughter coming from the kitchen. A woman's laughter. I pushed open the door to see Fenella sitting at the dining table.

"Morning, Nick. There's a hot pot of coffee on and I've made a stack of pancakes." She pointed to the worktop where indeed there was quite a pile and some syrup, sugar, and lemons. Judging by the state of my father who was rubbing his stomach as if in pain, I guessed he'd indulged in one too many. If Fenella stayed around it looked like my dad might begin to take on the appearance of the stereotypical Santa with his fat tum after all.

"Mmm, smells delicious," I said, taking in a nose-full of the scent of pancakes in the air, mixing in with the aroma of coffee. I didn't get chance to walk over to the worktop, as Fenella had already jumped up and told me to sit at the table. She faffed over me just like she'd done when I was a kid, giving me a plate full of pancakes and a large mug full of coffee. "OMG, can you move in?" I quipped, but as both Fenella and my father looked at the floor as they both went red, I realised it had been the wrong thing to say, and now I knew that they were both crushing on each other. Hmm, it might be time to temporarily step into my future role and perform my own Christmas miracle this season.

I spent the morning helping in the workshop and was so full that I actually turned down lunch. Fen had made a hamper full of sandwiches, quiches, and sausage rolls. My dad had gone from ruddy faced to looking a bit green when she'd told him. With my own potentially green-faced prospects ahead of me, I said bye, and made my way to the address that Chantelle had texted me.

Tree Root Walk was a small lane off the main Gnarly housing. It took me around twenty minutes to walk there from my house and that included me being slower as I was still so full, along with the fact that Alicia's house was at the end of a good five-minute walk down the lane.

I'd never had reason to come down here, so I was rather surprised to find a glass fronted modern home where I'd stereotypically expected a dark building surrounded by black cats. An attractive brunette answered the door.

"Nick, right?"

"Now I could be a delivery driver or a salesperson," I quipped, surprising myself by being a little flirtatious.

"Not with how Chantelle described you." She looked me up and down. "No, there's no doubt in my mind that you're Nick Anderson. Come on in. I'm Alicia."

I followed her through to a state-of-the-art kitchen where Chantelle sat on a stool at the gloss white kitchen island. "Hey, Nick. How are you?"

"Good, now I'm not inhabited by a dead spirit, and here's hoping you can make sure that doesn't happen again."

"Do you fancy a drink?" Alicia said and for a split-second I thought she was asking me on a date until I spotted the very expensive coffee maker on the countertop.

"A strong latte would be great thanks."

Chantelle giggled. "Are you still recovering from last night?"

"Last night?" Alicia said, looking between us both for an explanation. She definitely seemed interested.

"That's where I saw Nick. At the bistro. He was there with my friend, Dela."

"Oh?"

Was it me or did Alicia look disappointed? And how did I feel about that? Because while my first instinct was to declare myself unavailable given my feelings for Dela, hadn't the woman herself told me clearly that she wouldn't date me? So then why would I turn down a chance to enjoy time with the attractive woman here?

"Yes, we have Dela as a mutual friend. That's how I knew to ask Chantelle for help."

"Ah," Alicia replied looking less sullen. She turned then and started to fix my drink.

"So are you working later or is this a day off?" I asked Chantelle, thinking I'd better start concentrating on my visit and not the owner of the property.

"Day off, thank goodness. It gets a little crazy working at the bistro, being a witch, and helping care for my family."

"That does sound busy," I said politely.

"Yup. I have to help my mum with the triplets. They're a lot of work for her at forty-five years old, and now being the oldest of seven..."

"Means a lot of the responsibility falls on you.

Don't forget to remind your mum you're busy too though."

"Yeah, that doesn't work out so well for Chantelle seeing as she's responsible for the triplets in the first place." Alicia passed me my drink and raised a brow.

"Oh?"

"My mum said she was done with children, so I did a spell asking the power of three: that is the maiden, the mother, and the crone, but somehow I mixed things up and she ended up with triplets."

And this was the woman I was letting loose on my body?

I looked at my watch. "Do you know, I think actually I don't have time for this today." I hopped down off the bar stool I'd sat on.

Alicia laughed. "You're perfectly safe. Chantelle is my trainee now and has come on in leaps and bounds. She now makes very few errors and those she does, I correct while she's under my watch. Finish your drink and then we'll go through to my spell room."

I nodded, though I was still not entirely convinced.

CHAPTER FOURTEEN

Dela

That night in bed thinking about my rather fabulous kiss with Nick, I came to a decision...

I needed a date and fast. Thursday, no matter what else the day held, I would get on Tinder and line up a whole host of eligible men. That would help me feel more positive about my new home, would take my mind off Nick and his delectable lips and... sorry, my mind wandered off for another minute there... what was I saying? Oh yes, dates. Lots and lots of dates and less time thinking about the kiss.

I was glad to be spending my morning at the café where I fully expected to be distracted by the antics of Merrin and Aria as they got the bookstore and café ready.

Oh bugger, Thursday and Friday I'd have to work to show Aria the ropes, and also, there was the bookstore side of things. My sister had closed the place for the week, but it wasn't fair to leave her training Aria on her return. I'd bloody kill Mya if she wasn't already dead. How was I supposed to set up dates if I was working in a café that now would also have a bookshop?

I went to sleep and had fervent dreams of trying to kiss Nick and other men standing in my way.

"Wow," I said as I arrived at the building to find it was completed.

"We got here super early given none of us sleep much," Zane said. "Figured we could then leave the rest of you guys to do the décor. Everything else is done and dry."

"I just can't believe how fast you get things done."

"Believe it, because your house is next. Those plans are about to become real."

"If they go through."

"They'll go through." Zane smiled. "And when your sister comes back, she won't be the only one with a new place."

My competitive instinct rose then. I needed my place to be better than Callie's. It was stupid, but although her apartment would be amazing, she wouldn't have the gorgeous view of the woodland that I had.

And yes, it would be quiet out there, but hadn't I craved some quiet when the twins started nattering in stereo or in their experiments not to?

I would no longer be sharing a home. No one to nag me about housework and general tidying up, asking me to help out at the café. I would be free.

Not only that. I could sneak men back to my place and the gossips of Gnarly wouldn't know because it was out in the woods. I could make as much noise as I wanted.

No one would know if it was a serial killer. No one would hear your screams as you died.

My inner voice was a real buzz kill. It could sod off though as I finally realised how good having my own place would be. My stomach fizzed with the possibilities available once I had my own home.

Ignoring my inner ramblings, I beamed at Zane. "I can't wait. My own place for Christmas. And the house being huge means it'll fit in a giant Christmas tree."

"You'll also be able to string lights from the trees surrounding the place. I think it will look truly magical out there, Dela. Big place to hold a family Christmas too."

"There's only Callie and I, and now Lawrie."

"And me," Ginny said, making me startle in surprise as she came up behind me. "And probably Bernard and Aria would come, and those weird twin friends of yours. Family isn't just blood you know?"

"Okay, I'm off. You have my number if you need anything," Zane said, and I bid him farewell.

"What are you doing here?" I asked Ginny.

"Aria told me about the place being decorated today and her working here, so I came to check things out. You're here for Callie, so I thought I'd come knowing what my brother likes."

"Come on then, let's go in, because I'm half an hour late. I'm guessing Aria and Merrin are already making decisions and getting the place ready."

The windows had been covered in newspaper in order that no one outside got a sneak peek of the interior, and so when I opened the door I was pleasantly surprised to see all the cupcake bakery side of things was finished and not much different to how it had been before. Callie would appreciate that. Her displays were the same, it was just the pinks that had been muted by the new wall colours.

At the other side Merrin had clearly roped in Nick's friend Jason to help as they were carrying tables into the book zone.

Ginny walked over. "What's this old shit?"

Merrin put down the table and stood up to his full height, his dark eyes becoming small dots in his face as they narrowed on Ginny. He turned to me. "I told you she wouldn't like it."

Ah, he'd been talking about Ginny when he went weird before.

"I didn't know you knew Ginny," I said.

"Who is this idiot?" she asked.

"Ginny, this is Merrin, an artist, who also customises our recyclables. We've already agreed on the look and trust me, it's going to be fabulous."

"There's no point in trying to explain it to her. She's not from Gnarly and doesn't get the ethos. She wants everything new and shiny. Doesn't want to pay for it herself though. Wants some other poor bastard to pay. He'll pay all right." He stared at her. "Unearthly torture through listening to your constant demands."

"Merrin! That's uncalled for. Apologise at once,"

I said. "And also, you were wrong. She isn't working here."

"She will do. She'll lose her job at the inn at the same time as the other one will fall with child. Next June. It all kicks off next June."

"Who is this weirdo, and what is he talking about? Aria is extremely unlikely to get pregnant. Vampire births are rare."

"The transit of Venus awaits. The universe will align and bless with miracles," Merrin carried on.

"Can it bless us early with your mouth closing?" Ginny hissed at him.

"Okay, I think we'll let Merrin get on with unpacking all the furniture," I said as Aria appeared.

"Oh hey, you two. Have you come to help?"

"Yes, Ginny kindly volunteered to help me unpack and organise upstairs, didn't you, Ginny?" I grabbed her arm and nipped. She might be a strong vampire but being a younger sister, I'd learned to nip Callie when she'd been too bossy as a kid.

She jerked her arm out of my reach, wrinkling her nose up as her gaze alighted once more on Merrin. "Message received and understood. I couldn't possibly be around this rude man any longer anyway."

"Truth hurts," Merrin said with disdain and then

he went out of the back with Jason who had watched the exchange with amusement.

"What was that all about?" Aria asked.

"That weirdo has taken an instant dislike to me and started going on about me working here next June, something about Venus. Total crackpot."

"He is an acquired taste, but he's actually a nice man when you get to know him," Aria countered.

"Huh, well I won't be getting to know him," Ginny said. "I'll be upstairs when you're ready, Dela."

I shrugged my shoulders at Aria, told her I'd be upstairs if needed, and then I followed Ginny.

"How come you didn't tell Aria what Merrin said about a baby?" I asked.

"Because he's cuckoo. Vampire women crave children and most adopt a child turned in error or by the wild ones, but this happens little, and we're not allowed to turn a human child just for the sake of our maternal cravings. It would be cruel to let Aria believe she might get pregnant and for it to be nothing but the verbal diarrhoea of a madman."

"Fair enough. Merrin has said a lot of things that have come true though."

"We shall find out in June. If Aria is pregnant and I am working here in June, then I will believe it.

Until then I'd appreciate it if you would say no more. If the crazy dude tells her himself, that's up to him, but I won't tell her."

"I won't either. I agree. It would be cruel if it didn't come to pass."

With that we set to unboxing all my sister's belongings and then Ginny went back to the Letwine mansion and sent the rest of Lawrie's stuff through the portals. I made my excuses to go to meet Sheridan and left Ginny happily organising in a place where there wasn't a rude zombie.

I was just on my way to grab a slice of takeaway pizza when my phone rang, and Chantelle came on the line.

"Hi, Chantelle. Everything okay, or have you turned Nick into a frog?"

"Not yet I haven't, but I want to know if you want me to?"

"What?"

"Nick is here at Alicia's with me. We're about to go through to do the protection spell, but they are flirting with each other, and I thought you were interested in him."

I froze in place. Nick was flirting with this other woman, when I'd kissed him last night? Though it made no sense at all I was gutted that it clearly hadn't meant anything to him. Maybe when I'd kissed him, he'd decided there was no spark between us after all?

"No, we're just friends. I keep telling you that."

"You keep telling me that you won't date him because he's from Gnarly when clearly you fancy him. Why do you think I've not had a go at dating him myself? I saw your face when I was talking to him at the bar. You looked like you wanted to club Nick over the head, bang your chest and claim him as your own."

"I did not."

"You can deny it to yourself all you want, but not to me. Anyway, I need to get back, so my question is: do you want me to *accidentally* spell him to repel Alicia when she's not looking, or not?"

"Not. He can date who he likes."

"Okay, don't say I didn't warn you when you see him sticking his tongue down her throat and wish it were you."

I heard a female voice in the background. "I'm just finishing up here. On my way," Chantelle told them, and I bristled at realising the voice belonged to this *Alicia*. "Gotta go, bye," she said, and the call ended.

I didn't bother with any pizza then, finding I'd

lost my appetite. Instead, I walked to the entrance of the park, sat on the nearest bench, and waited for Sheridan to arrive. I put my arms around myself because it was so cold today, but also it felt like a hug, and I felt like I really needed one. At that point I missed my sister so much I could have cried. But as Sheridan arrived, I took a deep inhale, mentally dusted myself off, and got up to greet her.

CHAPTER FIFTEEN

Dela

Five years earlier...

It was done. At twenty-two and twenty-three years old, we'd had as much as we could stand of our parents' inability to acknowledge we were fae. It was heart-breaking, but when you were told if you refused to live as a human, you were disinherited, then the only thing to do was to walk away, and so that's what we'd done.

And now we sat on a platform at the train station, with suitcases and bags carrying what we could, but with no clue about where to go.

"How could they expect us to live a human life when our aging would slow down, not to mention any children we had would be half-fae if we married

human men?" I'd asked Callie a series of similar questions over the last few hours.

"Dela, they put their head in the sand and it was always going to lead to this moment. They couldn't adopt human children because they were too old and for whatever reason the fae placed us with them. We were brought up in a safe environment and we were loved."

"Loved as humans." I bristled. "How they could look upset as they told us we had to leave if we wanted to be our true selves is unbelievable."

"I know. But I understand, because they're clearly scared of what our fae heritage means."

As we'd grown older, Callie and I had gone into libraries and researched on the internet about our wings and worked out we were fae. Our under-standing of what exactly that meant was clunky though with no-one to ask.

"So, do you think that maybe if we find out more about ourselves and go back to see them, and they see we aren't really any different, they might think again?"

*Callie shook her head vigorously. "No. We **will** change because we **are** different. They've had their chance, and they chose to never see us again if we wanted to be our true selves. As far as I'm concerned,*

I'm through with them. They got the children they wanted, but I'm being the adult I want to be."

"Me too," I agreed. "You're so right. So now what?"

"Now, I call the number Mum, I mean Erica, gave me."

"She gave you a number? When?"

"She came in while I was packing my things. Said she was sorry and passed me the paper. Told me to take care of us both. That was it."

"Call it then."

The phone call led to us being told to get on a train to the centre of London where we were met at St Pancras by a slender, willowy woman, who looked in her mid-thirties. She introduced herself as Sheridan, a fae, and directed us to follow her to the taxi rank, after which we ended up in an exclusive looking salon, being served tea and coffee out of the finest bone china and choosing delectable cake, buns, and pastries from an elaborate cake stand that a waitress had brought and placed in the centre of the table. Callie chose a cupcake with whirls of pink strawberry frosting and real strawberry pieces. She devoured it while I picked at a piece of flapjack, not feeling hungry for anything other than information and a feeling of security.

"I'm terribly sorry that your place with the Fran-

cis' has come to such an abrupt end, but it is not unusual for fostered or adopted fae. Human parents swear blind that they will do anything in order to have a child, but once the child-rearing is done and they can no longer escape the fact their children are not human, a lot either seek our support, or they do as your parents have, and decide to issue ultimatums which lead to separation. Anyway, before we go on, I just want to let you know that we have funds for such occurrences and I will be setting you up in a new home, so don't be worrying about bed and board, okay? Let's get that out of the way straight off."

Both Callie and I visibly relaxed at knowing that no matter what else happened, this woman would give us a place to stay. We could survive anything as long as we were together, but being together, safe, and warm was even better.

"Thank you," I said, suddenly feeling like I could eat my flapjack after all.

Sheridan told us to eat and drink and that there was plenty of time to get to where we'd be staying, so we relaxed a little, enjoying the warmth and comfort of the posh establishment. My sister seemed in awe of it, looking around at the décor which I personally found over-the-top, all mirror balls, large mirrors, and frilly tablecloths. Then again, Callie had been the girly girl who loved her dolls and I'd been the younger sibling who loved sneaking out to meet boys. I'd pretended to like football, but really, I'd liked the players.

As we'd got older, we'd both dated, but there had never been anyone significant, and our parents had never put pressure on us, possibly because they knew it would have led to the inevitable—facing up to our faeness.

"Can you tell us anything about our parents? Are they still alive?" Callie asked, having eaten her fill of food. She'd wiped her mouth on the cloth napkin, set it down, and now wore her serious face.

"I can't unfortunately at present. Yes, they are alive. I can tell you that much. But for reasons I can't go into at present, I can't tell you about them." She looked at our faces. "I know it's not what you want to hear, but I can tell you about your heritage."

She went on to explain that we were tooth fairies.

"You were born in the woodland of a place called Gnarly Fell. No one knew your mother was pregnant with you, Callie, and who the father was, and so she found a place that had been abandoned by the fae many hundreds of years before but was still fae ground. They went from there and kept travelling to a new abandoned dwelling and then returned to the same place in Gnarly to have you, Dela, until one day their pasts caught up with them. They were forced to find a new place for you both and that's when they discovered the Francis'."

"So they couldn't keep us. Did they want to?" I asked.

"It's so very complicated that it's best I say no more," Sheridan answered.

"I'll take that as a no then," I said. "It's fine. We don't need anyone else, do we, Callie? We have each other."

"Maybe one day, they'll—"

Callie held up her hand. "No. We're in our twenties and they haven't contacted us since they left us with the Francis'. Dela is right, we don't need our fae parents. We're very grateful to you, Sheridan, for meeting us, being a contact, and for providing support and accommodation, but if you take us to where we need to stay, we'll be fine from there. We'll find our own way."

And that's what had happened. We'd entered Gnarly, got permission to reside there given our birth story, and been shown the apartment over a vacant shop building. Sheridan had said all we had to do to *earn our keep was to provide service as a tooth fairy by baking goods and sending them to the headquarters. In return, we'd be given a healthy allowance that meant we wouldn't worry for money. Callie had immediately said she wanted to take over the building downstairs and open a café.*

Once permissions were in place from Gnarly's council for us to officially reside there, Sheridan had left.

Callie and I had been determined to not ever rely on anyone else other than each other. She had thrown herself into her business, and I'd thrown myself at men, looking for fun and not anything serious.

"Hi, Sheridan. Thanks for coming to see me," I said, giving her a warm hug. We'd spoken to her on the telephone infrequently, but just knowing she was there had helped us enormously until we'd settled into the fell.

She hugged me back heartily. She didn't look any different from the last time we'd seen her, five years before, and yet I'd aged to close the gap. I wondered how old she really was, given the fae tended to slow right down after the age of thirty. It wasn't like I was used to seeing other fae to hazard a guess.

"You're looking really well, Dela. So are we staying in the park or going to enjoy a cupcake?"

"Hmm, about that," I replied, and I filled her in on the latest developments. "But we could go look at the place where my new home is going to be built?" I suggested.

"Sure, let's do that, and we can chat on the way," she said.

We took a slow stroll and at first exchanged pleasantries. "And so have you had time to think more about why you're asking questions about your parentage?" Sheridan eventually asked.

"It's just the right time."

"But you might anger Callie by finding out. You've always been such a rock to the other. I'd hate to think you would jeopardise that by finding out. Why not wait until she's back from honeymoon and sound things out with her?" Sheridan observed me, her brows drawn together.

"No. Callie has made her choices and in fact, has made a lot of choices for me in the past. And that's fine. In some ways it's not been fair to her that I've allowed her to do that. She's had to suffer my moods because there was no parent there. Sometimes she's had to be the parent. But she's married now, and our relationship is changing. It's going to evolve more. We'll always be close, but we won't be so dependent on the other. And no matter what the truth about our parents, I need to know it. Even if it means I still don't meet them, or have a relationship with them, I want to know the story of where we came from. Of who birthed me and then gave me away. I need to know why so that I can move on myself."

"Okay. I understand that," Sheridan responded. "You understand why I had to ask?"

"I do. But I'm ready."

"I can see that, and now I will tell you how you came to be adopted. Shall we carry on strolling or would you rather we sat?"

"Let's keep walking."

Sheridan nodded and then began to tell me about my parentage.

"Your mother was a servant of the royal court, a very low-ranking servant, and one day, up early to mop the floors, she was on her way to get some clean water when she found the eldest prince stuck halfway through a window. She helped him and he was so grateful he began to smuggle luxury items to her, such as leftover meat and cake from the banquets. He'd bring them in the late evening on his way to his secret excursions. The prince confessed to her that he went to bars at night pretending to be a normal fae. He'd wear an enchantment so no one recognised him. The royals had access to the strongest witches and wizards and money bought silence. He confessed that his visits to her were cloaked and would arouse no suspicion even though she shared a dorm with five others. No one ever woke when she went to meet the prince."

I was unable to speak. Our mother and a prince? Secretly meeting in the palace?

"They'd sit in a small study room and talk for hours. Eventually talking led to other things and she found herself pregnant."

"We're half-royal?" I gasped, coming to a stop.

Sheridan seemed weighed down by the story she was telling. Though we'd been walking slowly it was like she was carrying the burden of it on her shoulders, and I guessed there wasn't going to be a happy ending to this tale.

"Sorry, continue," I said, and I carried on strolling.

"When she told the prince, she said she planned to run away. That she knew he couldn't admit to being the father and that as long as he could obtain safe passage for her through enchantments and spells and she could have her baby, she would remember the love they had shared and pass it along to her child. But he refused. He said he loved her and they would escape together and that's what they did. They evaded the fae courts and ran to no longer used fae land, eventually having your sister. They were madly in love, until the enchantment vanished and they were caught."

"How did that happen?"

"The royal court had slowly questioned the magical society one by one until they believed they knew the culprit. And then they made sure by capturing his own children that the wizard had no choice but to give up his secrets. They threw him in jail and threw his wife and children out of the court altogether in punishment and to serve as a warning to any other sorcerers. The prince was told that if he agreed to return to the court and in time become king, then they could find someone to take care of the children. They would allow that. Your father agreed but insisted it would be with humans and only your mother would ever know who they were. He said he couldn't bear to know because he'd want to find you and it would torment him more to know than to not."

"That's so sad. So what happened to them after?" The tale was making my chest ache with the emotion as I imagined my parents faced with this impossible situation and having to let us, and each other go.

"They threw your mother in jail. She didn't protest and stopped your father from doing so on her behalf. She accepted the sentence as long as they promised to let her find you a home. And that's what happened. You were adopted, your father eventually became king, and your mother spent many years in prison."

We reached the clearing and I pointed to the space. "This is where my house will be."

Sheridan followed my pointing finger and then she staggered over and bent double. She looked in such severe discomfort that I fell to my knees, grabbing her shoulder, and attempting to see what the matter was.

"Are you ill? Do I need to call an ambulance?"

She shook her head, but her features were etched in pain and her voice cracked as she said. "That's exactly where you and your sister were born."

"Really? Oh wow. What are the chances, hey?" I said. "But don't get upset. I know it's not a happy ending, my father being king of a fae court and my mother in prison, but at least I know they really loved each other." I escorted her to the tree stump I'd sat on when I'd looked at the space with Nick. "So anyway, how did you get to know my mother and find out our story?"

But as I looked back at Sheridan I realised why, as that truth was etched all over her face.

"Oh my god. Are *you* our mother?" I asked.

But I didn't need her to answer. Not in the slightest.

CHAPTER SIXTEEN

Nick

We chatted while we finished our drinks and I found out that Alicia had only moved back to Gnarly a month ago and still spent a lot of time with the Manchester coven who she'd been with for the past ten years.

"The family home was a bit cliché, so I got some builders in to modernise," she explained.

"This place is seriously impressive, and that now explains why I haven't seen you around here much."

"I'm not a huge socialiser. I know there are always these group things happening in Gnarly, but it's not really my thing," Alicia explained. "In Manchester, I was able to live a relatively normal life, and just check in with the coven there periodically. It was nice." She looked wistful for a moment.

"So you had family here then?" I was being extremely nosy but new people had to be approved to come to the fell. Plus, she'd said 'family home', but there was no evidence of other people in the house, though they could have been at work I supposed.

"My father moved into a bungalow on Drop-leaf Lane. This place was too large for him. He's retired now."

"I have to say I've never been particularly aware of their being any witches or wizards around Gnarly, although I know I can't know everyone here," I acknowledged.

"That's the thing isn't it? Gnarly is small but it still doesn't mean you know everyone. You might see people in passing and say hi, and I'll bet you've seen my father many times, but yes, we tend to do our magic within larger covens. My father is with a London branch and my mother is with the Manchester one I was with until recently."

No doubt her parents' relationship had been another casualty of the Gnarly curse.

"I've just remembered a call I need to make. I won't be a moment," Chantelle said. I'd actually forgotten she was there. I'd been so engrossed in Alicia's family history, I think I'd forgotten why I was there too. She left the room.

"Okay, so this is a little forward of me, but I feel like we're getting on. Do you fancy having a drink in the new year?" Alicia asked. "I don't have any time before then, unfortunately."

I thought about the actual chances of Dela changing her mind and decided not to factor her into my decision making.

"Sounds good, and after the new year here too. I've a lot going on at the moment."

"Of course you will. You're the son of Santa himself. What was I thinking, saying I was busy. My plans will be nothing at the side of yours." She laughed. After a few minutes, she excused herself to go look for Chantelle.

They returned to the room and Chantelle looked at me. "Okay, are you ready?"

"As I'll ever be," I said, and I followed them to the spell room.

The room was painted cream. It had laminate wood flooring, and a large rug with a pentagram imprinted on it laid in the centre of the floor. I was asked to take a seat on the rug on one of the points and the two witches sat there too so that we were in a triangle.

Chantelle had brought a satchel with her and she rummaged through it and brought out a red candle, a small bottle of water, and a blue bowl that she filled with the water. She placed them at the other empty points and then began to speak.

"The pentagram points represent earth, air, fire, water, and spirit. Today, blessed goddess, I ask that you divine earth through Alicia who is a Capricorn, and air through our guest, Nick, who will concentrate on his breath throughout the process. I shall channel the spirit of our ancestors in order to perform today's protection spell."

I made sure to do as asked and to breathe in and out, concentrating on my inhale and exhale.

"You don't have to sound like you're in labour," Alicia whispered.

Feeling embarrassed, I made sure to breathe more quietly.

"May the elements unite and form a protective shield for our visitor here today, Stanley Nicholas Anderson. May no evil spirits be able to invade his body from here on out."

Coloured orbs came out from each other point. White from Chantelle's, Red from the candle, brown from Alicia's, blue from the water bowl. They met in the centre of the circle. Clear orbs met them that had come from the point I sat on. The colours swirled together until golden orbs shone and then they shattered into lots of tiny, glittery looking particles. They moved over and for a moment covered my body and then they were gone.

"I will now close the spell," Chantelle said.

Alicia shook her head. "Just a moment." She said an invocation and took a small twig from her pocket and placed it on the pentagram point. "This will hold my placc until I return." Then she left the room.

Chantelle and I sat in silence until she returned. I didn't want to speak in case it wasn't allowed, but it was really difficult not to ask what was going on.

When Alicia returned, she held a small bottle of whisky. Looked like we were celebrating. It was only early afternoon, but if it was part of the ritual then I'd partake. I did love a tipple of scotch.

Alicia handed it to me. "Drink this."

"All of it?"

"As much as you feel you are able," she said, with a smirk on her face.

Huh. Did she think I was a feeble drinker or something? I took the top off the bottle and raised it to my lips, opened my mouth, and... the liquid missed my mouth entirely and ran down my top. I tried again over and over to no avail.

"What's happening?" I said eventually, giving up.

"Evil spirits are unable to evade your body, and given alcohol has the ability to do harm to your body, right now you can't drink any."

"Oh," said Chantelle, looking sullen.

"Your spell was extremely well executed, Chantelle," Alicia encouraged. "It's just you must think of what you are asking and be very specific so that there is no room for error. Now let's do this again." Alicia quickly said a spell herself that removed the previous one and I watched the gold glitter work in reverse to form the orbs that sunk back into their points.

Chantelle repeated the whole spell but this time she asked, "May the elements unite and form a protective shield for our visitor here today, Stanley Nicholas Anderson. May no wayward spirits, no displaced entities, be able to invade his body from here on out."

Once more the orbs combined and the gold glitter sunk into my form. I reached for the whisky and took a sip.

"Perfect, Chantelle. Now you may close the circle," Alicia instructed.

"Earth, air, fire, water, and spirit. Thank you for your service here today. I am your loyal servant and I give my thanks to you working through me." She blew out the candle and picked it up, wafting the smoke around her. She then drank the water and touched Alicia and me on the shoulder before placing both her hands palm down onto the centre of the carpet. Silver sparks flew from her fingers and sank through the carpet.

"It is done," she said, and then she smiled.

Alicia assured me that I now had protection against any spirits or entities, evil or otherwise, trying to invade my body and that if my father wanted the same protection affording him, they were willing to drop into the workshop. I gave him a call and he'd said he'd be grateful for their protection and so we all walked back to mine, where I left the women with my father and returned to the house, having informed them they could draw a pentagram on the floor of our back yard.

After that, I found Fenella had left some of the sandwiches and quiche from earlier in the fridge. I ate and washed it all down with a cuppa and then I decided to have an afternoon nap, given that the evening might prove stressful and leave me with a lot to think about.

When I woke up, I looked at my phone while I came around. There was no reason why Dela should have messaged me, but I felt disappointed seeing nothing there. I decided to send her a message myself.

Nick: Hey, just a quickie to say I hope your meeting with the fae went okay.

I waited a while, but when I didn't receive a response, I made my way downstairs to get a drink and then I sat in the living room with the address book and worked out how to drive to my mother's house. I felt like I had a lump stuck in my throat and knew for a fact that the hours between now and when I set off were going to be like waiting for a painful operation. But there was nothing else to be done but to wait. I knew that my mind would not be distracted by helping my dad. I'd no doubt make a mistake and cause more harm than good trying to help him. I flicked through Facebook for a while and then just laid staring at the ceiling.

Eventually my phone pinged with a text.

Dela: I'll be at yours at seven.

That was all it said. Nothing about her meeting with the fae. A sinking feeling went through me. If it had gone well, she'd have said so. In fact, I'd have expected her to turn up chattering away about it all. Now that made me wonder if I was doing the right thing. Should I not contact my mother? Should I leave well alone?

I had another ninety minutes to sit and watch the clock go around and to deliberate over everything. I spent it daydreaming, imagining all the different scenarios that could happen: my mum not answering, her slamming the door in my face, her ringing a priest to perform an exorcism. You name it, I thought it, until eventually it was time for me to get ready. I'd not eaten anything else since I'd gotten back earlier because I couldn't face a thing.

Just before seven the doorbell rang and I went to the back door and came face-to-face with a stony-faced Dela.

"Hey."

"Nick, are you sure about this?" she said.

I grabbed my coat and locked the door behind me, heading to the seating area. "What's going on? I'm guessing today didn't go well."

Tears welled in her eyes.

"Oh, Dela, what happened?" I asked moving to put an arm around her. But she flinched and moved away from me.

"Don't."

I felt like she'd slapped me but had to remind myself that this was Dela. Blocked off and unwilling to uncover any vulnerability. My guess was that her efforts to put herself out there about her parentage had not worked and so now her armour was back in place.

"I don't want to talk about it right now. I will, but not now. I need to think about something else, focus on your journey. I just want to check with you that you know what you're doing before we set off because once you knock on that door, if she opens it, that's it. Anything could happen and no matter how much you've thought about it, nothing might prepare you for the truth."

My father came out then from the workshop. Dela schooled her features into 'normal Dela'. "Hey, Stan," she said. But my father scowled at her and ignored her. What was up with my dad?

"I'm getting ready to go to the council meeting," he said to me and then he went into the house.

"What was all that about?" Dela asked. "Did I do

something to offend him? He did give me side-eye didn't he? I wasn't imagining it?"

"He'll just be stressed at having to leave the workshop to go to the meeting. He'll have been in a dreamworld and not even noticed he scowled and ignored you," I said.

Dela seemed to accept me at my word, thank goodness.

"Right." I got my car keys out of my pocket and swung them between us. "Let's do this."

I drove us to the semi-detached house on Streatham Common and somehow managed to find a car parking space just further down the road from the house which was situated on a hill.

"Now what?" I said to Dela. "I don't have the first clue what to do. Do I just knock on the door, ask for Mo if someone else answers and then announce I'm her not-long-lost-just-unwanted son?"

Dela frowned and sat silent for a moment. Then she grabbed her bag. "No. We knock and pretend we're looking for someone and we have a good look at who answers while we are 'at the wrong house'."

It seemed a good a plan as any, so I got out of the car.

"I'll do the talking," Dela said, and I just nodded. I didn't think I could have spoken anyway. I felt frozen. Mute.

We walked up the small frontage of the house with its tiny amount of off-road parking. The semi looked relatively newly built. Dela rang the bell.

A young guy who looked in his mid-twenties answered. "Yeah?" He was dressed in jeans and a t-shirt, looked in need of a shave, and his eyes spent more time on Dela than on me.

"Hi, I'm looking for Chantelle and Jason, but I have a feeling now you've answered that I'm at the wrong house."

"Yeah, there's no-one of that name lives here. What address is it they gave you?"

"That's the thing. I didn't get the exact address off them because I'd been before."

"I told you to call them before we set off," I told her, starting to find my voice again and attempting to play my part.

"You didn't call them though, did you?" she shot back before turning around to the guy. "Brothers hey, who'd have them?"

Brother? She'd told him I was her brother.

The guy shrugged. "I don't have them, just a sister, but that's probably just as painful, if not worse. What were the names of the people you're looking for again? I'll go and ask my mum as she's home. She might know where they live."

But he didn't need to as his mum, *our* mum, came to the door. I looked at the woman who her son resembled so strongly in terms of his blonde colouring. The same colouring I shared too, except my facial features and body type were all my fathers. Everything except our eyes, which were so similar it was spooky and I saw that she'd registered this too, her pupils dilating.

"What's going on?" she said.

"These people are looking for a Chantelle and Jason..." He looked to Dela for a surname.

"Chantelle *Christmas* and Jason *Anderson*," I said. Just so she'd know for sure.

"Right, I'll leave you to it, Mum." The guy nodded at us both and left the doorway.

"I'm afraid I don't know anyone of that name. Sorry," Mo said. "Have you come far?"

"From a small village just outside central London. Not too far. We'll give them a ring anyway and see which is the exact house," Dela said. "I should have done that in the first place. Sorry for any inconvenience."

Her son re-appeared. "I'm going out now, Mum. I'll catch you later," he said to her. She told him goodbye and to have a good time and then as he passed, he knocked into Dela. "Sorry," he said, but I saw him pass her a folded piece of paper. Did he know more than he was letting on? Did he suspect who I was?

My mum waited until he'd gone out of view and then she said to me, "I knew one day you would come. You'd better come in."

And with that myself and then Dela made our way into my mother's home.

Dela

As I followed Nick into his mother's home, I slipped the piece of paper I'd just been handed inside my handbag. Nick's half-brother had whispered, "Call me," as he'd departed. If my life wasn't complicated enough right now.

I got a good look at a hideous, garish, striped carpet in white, beige and shit-brown. It looked like an infant had skidded down it without a nappy on. Take 'skidded' any way you liked, the movement or the result. Thankfully, the living room was much more subdued, the walls a pale-green colour. A beige carpet appeared in the small gaps between furniture. Mo indicated for us to take a seat, but she didn't ask if we wanted a drink. I got the impression we weren't welcome.

My eyes flicked over to the walls where there was a picture of the family together. It looked like it had been taken at a celebration as they were all dressed in their finest with a lake in the background. Nick's half-sister also had blonde hair, but then I saw that their father was blonde too.

"If you've come for a happy family reunion, you'll be disappointed," Mo said. I looked at Nick whose eyes widened.

"I just came because I wanted to meet the person who gave birth to me. I wanted to know the other half of the mix. See where I came from," he said quietly.

"Did your father not tell you I didn't want a relationship with you? I mean you're how old now?" She didn't say the age and it was almost like I could see where the barbs were hitting Nick as her disinterest became further apparent. For a tall, stocky guy he seemed to shrink before my eyes. And I'd had enough.

"We're here because Nick just wanted to meet you one time to find out about the other part of his DNA. He's already aware that you don't want contact with him; the thirty years you've ignored him attest to that. But if you could find the common courtesy to afford us a few minutes of your time right now, so that he can get some answers in order to move on with his life, I'd appreciate it."

"And you are?" she said snootily.

"I'm his *wife*, and we want to have children and so need to know his heritage," I spat out. Nick almost fell off the sofa. "The quicker you talk instead of sitting there looking at him like he's the shit on your shoe the better. Not because we'll be gone, but because you're in danger of me going nuclear and given I'm a demon maybe you don't want that?" It was another lie, but as I saw fear lick across her eyes, it made me feel better. Not so high and fucking mighty now, was she?

"Fine. I'll tell you what you need to know and then you can leave," she said to us both. "There are no health issues from my family except some eczema and you'd have suffered with that by now if you were going to get it. Otherwise, my family have lived to a ripe old age, *unfortunately*." Her lips puckered. "I met your father and was just after a bit of fun. It was fine until he started going on about being Father Christmas. I thought, typical, get a good lay and he turns out to be whacko. When I found I was pregnant, I didn't tell him because I wanted to keep my distance from the nutjob. I did however realise it could get me a flat and benefits, so I kept you."

I wanted to punch her in the nose, but figured if I did that, Nick wouldn't get the rest of the story of his birth and mother, so I refrained. I did however have to sit on my hands while she carried on talking.

"A few days after your birth I walked into your bedroom and found an elf there. I thought I was delusional—postpartum psychosis I put it down to. Looked it up on the internet. Except your dad had told me hadn't he that he was Father Christmas... I told myself I was going crazy now, but he'd told me about the tucked away village where you lived and so I decided to find him.

"And that was that. I left you with your father. The supernatural one of us. I returned to my life, thankful that no elves visited again, and neither did I have a crying, wailing baby around which hadn't been the meal ticket I'd thought it would be. Eventually, I married my now husband, who although not a millionaire had enough money to provide me with a nice house and comfort and when I had my kids I also had a nanny. Plus, knowing they were fully human things were just better."

"And my siblings have no clue about me?" Nick asked.

"As far as I'm concerned, they never will."

Mo had an ugly twist to her mouth and I wasn't

giving her chance to tell us to get out. "Okay, we're done here," I said, and I indicated for Nick to stand up. "You got anything else to say, Nick, before we leave?"

Nick put his hands in his pockets and it took him a while to look up from the floor. When he did, his eyes held an inward, pained look. "I'm sorry you couldn't deal with me being different, but I thank you for dropping me back with my father, because that was the right choice and I've had an amazing childhood." As he spoke, he crossed his arms over his chest and straightened up, like every word gave him inner strength. "So thank you for birthing me and thank you for giving me up."

Mo clearly had been expecting an insult rather than his thanks because she nodded and dropped her defences.

"It was the right decision, Stanley. For both of us."

He nodded back. "You can be rest assured that I won't be in contact again."

He walked off towards the door, but I didn't follow. Instead, I turned to his mother. "Nick is different, but he has the hugest heart, and it has been for the best you giving him to his father, because maybe if you hadn't, he'd have ended up bitter and twisted like you. I don't know what your own story is and why you don't seem to have a loving attachment to your own parents, but for God's sake I hope you tell your two other children you love them, so they don't continue to pass down your shallowness. I know for a fact that Nick will shower our own children with so much love they'll find it cringeworthy but adorable, and they'll shine bright from knowing just how much he loves them." I walked off then out to the car where I promptly burst into tears, before taking a number of deep breaths and wiping my face on the back of my hands. Because it was true. Nick would make an amazing father, and I was starting to think my rule for not dating Gnarly residents was stupid.

"Okay, when I get home, I'm drinking," Nick said. "Want to join me? We'll sit outside near the patio heater, and you can tell me what happened to you today, because that's twice you've got emotional and tried to shrug it off now, and enough's enough. We need to face up to our pasts, Dela."

I nodded because I couldn't trust myself to speak, not while I was so emotional. I couldn't make decisions about Nick while I had such big decisions to make about my parents. Alcohol and talking sounded like a good combination, as long as I didn't drink too much. As I was working tomorrow morning, I'd keep an eye on my intake. Just enough to not have any more fucks to give was the right alcoholic units for this evening.

We travelled back not saying much, both of us deep in thought and Nick concentrating on the unfamiliar roads. When we got back, he parked up and we both exited the car.

"If you follow me in, you can sit in the kitchen until I've got the heater going and the blankets out. You can help get the drinks and snacks sorted."

Nick was outside placing a couple of big blankets out there and I was making two hot toddies when Stan came back. He said something to Nick and patted his arm comfortingly. I knew Stan wouldn't be surprised at the outcome of Nick meeting his mother. After a few minutes I then saw Nick's face light up before he turned around in my direction and raised his voice. "Dela, you got permission for your house. It's happening. You're getting your new home in Gnarly."

I ran outside. "Really. Oh thank you, Stan. Thanks so much."

He'd been so loving towards his son, but then Stan turned to me and all emotion slipped away. "It wasn't me; it was the council. The secretary will email your permissions tonight so that building can start in the morning." He then turned back to Nick. "Good night, son," he said. "I'd better see what's been happening in my absence. I'll catch up with you tomorrow."

Once more he dismissed me. No good night, no smile. I had definitely done something to offend him. Only I could fall out with Father Christmas. I guess it was connected to his son. Maybe he felt I was using Nick and messing him around.

"I've upset your father in some way. I'm just going to have a chat with him." I took a step towards the workshop.

"No." Nick blocked my way. "I don't know what's up with my dad, but I'll talk to him. Meanwhile, you can sit here and tell me about what happened this afternoon. That's more important than my dad being a bit off. He was probably just annoyed that the council meeting put him behind in his work."

"Maybe," I replied, but I didn't feel either of us was convinced given this was the second time he'd been cool and dismissive of me in one day.

Having a drink, I recounted the story of that afternoon, of seeing Sheridan and her revealing that she was our mother, and about the fact the house was being built on the exact area where Callie and I had both been born.

"Anyway, she was so upset that it was basically impossible to speak to her about things any further. We agreed that I needed time to think about what she'd said and also to speak to Callie about it. So I know where she is when I'm ready to talk and find out more."

"And what about your father?"

"As far as we'd got was that my father was now king of a royal court. Which one I don't know and I'm sure he's not going to want two illegitimate children appearing anyway. I don't know how Sheridan got out of prison either."

"You must have so many questions?"

"I do, but she's right. We both have a lot to think about, and I want to give my sister the opportunity to find out more if she wishes. She'll be back Saturday. I've waited this long to find out, a few more days waiting won't hurt."

"Callie's coming back to quite the few surprises, a new shop and home, and parents." Nick's gaze was probing.

I shrugged my shoulders. "The whole past couple of weeks have been a huge shock for us both, a couple more shocks won't hurt. Might as well come at her like a giant plaster to pull off at once."

He huffed. "At least she'll find out she has a mother that loves her."

I nodded. "Yeah, it's more than we had before. Well, we had a caring woman who loved us in her own way."

"Even that though. Yes, your human parents made you make a choice, but they're bound to have been scared. Look at what mine said about getting home and elves being in my bedroom. I wonder if thinking of you embracing your true selves was just too frightening a prospect for them, rather than a rejection of you. They raised you to your twenties after all."

"Maybe, but I believe that door is closed. They won't change their minds and if they did choose to do so, they have Sheridan's number. The first move would need to come from them."

"I get that. Want another?" Nick said, pointing to my drained glass.

"Yes please and then I'd better head home as it's the first day of the new café tomorrow."

"Are you having an opening celebration?" he asked while he took my glass from me.

"No, I'll leave that to Callie. Doesn't seem fair to

do it without her and if she hates it and makes Mya return it all back to how she left it, it would be even more embarrassing."

"Okay, we need to drink a toast to your new home. Tomorrow I'll be helping with the foundations." Nick stood up and went into the house to make us new hot toddies and I took the opportunity to go see what his father's issue with me was.

I pushed open the door of the workshop and saw Stan talking to an elf. As he caught my eye, he dismissed the elf and gave me an eye roll.

"What do you want?" he said rudely, wearing a hard expression on his features.

It took me a moment to formulate a response because I was crestfallen. Dismissed and disliked by Santa. It made every miserable Christmas look like a winning lottery ticket at the side of him not liking me.

"I-I'm not sure what I've done, Stan, but I can only think it's to do with Nick and maybe you think I'm messing him around..."

"Well, aren't you?" he snapped.

I felt my chin quiver. *Oh God, don't cry in front*

of Santa, Dela, be strong. I swallowed, though my mouth was dry. "I like Nick a lot, b-but I have a rule that I don't date men from Gnarly. He's a really good friend to me, and I to him though, so please, is there any way we can form a truce, you and I, so that things aren't awkward when we're both around Nick?" My body shook as I awaited his response, my breath held for a moment.

Stan smirked. It was very confusing.

"Oh, yes, let's call a truce, and ooh, do you think you could approach Nick the same way you have me should you date and it not work out? I mean surely making a truce with the lovely Nick Anderson wouldn't be half as painful as having to make one with Santa Claus?"

My mouth fell open. Then I folded my arms across my chest and cocked my hip. "You mean this was all a ruse? This ignoring me and making me feel shitty?'

"Yup," he said, and he started laughing. "Ho ho ho, ho ho ho."

"It's not funny," I said, standing there with my hands on my hips and giving him side-eye. And then I thought about what he'd said and realised that he was right, and I no longer had to keep myself away from dating Nick.

Rules were stupid.

Truces were clever. Santa was even cleverer. I grabbed his arm, kissed him on the cheek, and saying, "Thanks, Father Christmas," I then ran out of the workshop, hearing his giggles getting further away.

CHAPTER EIGHTEEN

Nick

I came out of the house with the drinks and Dela was gone. If her bag hadn't still been on the seat, I might have thought she'd left, but it appeared she'd gone to see my father in the workshop after all. I didn't know what was going on with him and why he was being so rude to her, and I resolved to have a word with him myself if she came out none the wiser. While I waited, I placed the drinks on the table and sat back in front of the heater.

But when she left the workshop, she came out smiling. She thanked the elf who'd held the door open for her. There was a huge beam across her face, and her hands were behind her back.

"Stand up," she ordered. "I have your Christmas present for you. Come on, hurry."

I stood up.

"Now close your eyes."

I did as asked.

And then footsteps came nearer. I held out my hands and Dela took them in her own, pulling them around her body.

My own eyes shot open and I stared down into hers. "I-I don't understand."

Dela winked at me. "I'm your present, dummy. If things don't work out, we'll call a truce, okay? Go back to being friends or at least civil, so that Gnarly isn't ruined as my home. Deal?"

"Are you being serious? You're breaking your rule?"

"Breaking, forgetting, regretting I ever made i—"

I cut her off with a kiss. My head lowered to hers, hers tilted up to mine. I placed my hand under her chin softly and placed my lips on hers. I'd imagined this moment for so long and the reality didn't disappoint. When I broke off, I knew I had to ask the question.

"Are you sure about this?"

She grabbed my hand and started pulling me towards my back door.

"I'm sure."

The drinks were left outside to go cold, as we

made our way into the warmth, though Dela shivered as I caressed her skin as I finally got her naked. Slipping beneath the sheets I couldn't believe this was really happening as our limbs tangled together. I couldn't get enough of her kisses and of the feel of her body both to my fingers, my tongue, and of my skin next to her skin. Dela's needy little pants showed me she was feeling the same way and when she finally begged me to get inside her, I was more than ready to do so.

We moved together, my hand in her hair and Dela's hand squeezing my butt.

"Open your eyes," I commanded, and she did. We stared at each other as our pace quickened and as we both fell over the edge.

Afterwards, Dela spent time tracing my tattoos as we remained curled around each other.

"Now I'm really annoyed with myself for wasting so much time. To think I've been denying myself access to this magnificent cock all this time," she said, her fist curling around my dick.

"Well, we have the rest of the evening to do some catching up." I wiggled my brows at her, and we did indeed do exactly that.

When I woke the next morning, were it not for the warm body wrapped around my own, I would have thought the whole thing a dream.

"You even snore cute," Dela said, her hand stroking down my chin. "Good morning."

"It's a very good morning. I can't believe you're here and this is happening," I confessed.

"Well, it would seem there are more than three wise men at Christmastime," she answered. "And one of those pointed out to me that even if things didn't work out and we no longer got along, it could still be amicable."

"So that's what my dad was up to."

"Yup, and it made me think. Because I care for your father, and it hurt when he was ignoring me. But I went in the workshop to ask why he was being mean to me and asking if we could form a truce, and that's when he pointed out that if I kept that philosophy, I could break my rule. So now." She started giggling. "I can date all the men in Gnarly too."

I grabbed her and pulled her underneath me. "You'll have to escape my bed first. Go on, try it." I held her hands above her head.

"I don't want to escape," she said while wriggling her hips. My morning hard-on could no longer be ignored as she writhed against it, and as I looked down at her naked breasts, neither could her amazing body. I looked at the clock. There was still time before either of us needed to get to work, but to be honest, if there hadn't been, we just would have been late.

My father and Fenella were both absent from the kitchen when Dela and I finally made our way downstairs. I reckoned my dad had pulled an all-nighter. "What can I get you to drink and eat?" I asked.

"Oh I think I've eaten plenty this morning." She winked. "Anyway, I have an idea. Come with me to the shop and I'll make us some break-fast. You can be my first customer, with extra-special privileges in getting to come in before it opens."

"Thank goodness for that because I'm hopeless in the kitchen," I confessed.

"That's okay. You make up for it elsewhere." She grinned.

I grinned right back because right now Dela was my...? Was she?

"Are you my girlfriend now, Dela, or just my secret lover?"

"Super, red-hot girlfriend, I reckon. Don't you?"

I pushed her up against the kitchen wall to let her know how much I liked her answer.

As the shop appeared in the distance it was really quite remarkable that the makeover for it had taken just days. The building still fit in with those around it, but it was now doubled in size and the pink signage with black writing stated *Books and Buns*. Underneath it said, ***Eating and reading are two pleasures that combine admirably* – C.S. Lewis**. Dela told me that Aria had suggested the quote, and I agreed that it couldn't have been more perfect. We went inside and said hello to the lady herself who was already there, along with Lawrie's sister.

"Hey," we said as we walked in.

"Hey," Aria replied as Ginny waved. "I figured

we could use an extra pair of hands today, so I dragged Ginny here."

"As long as I don't have to see the great undead and unwashed, I'll be fine," Ginny declared and Aria and Dela shared a look.

"What's all that about?" I whispered.

"Merrin. I'll tell you about it later. They do not get on," Dela said.

"Nick, I know you're distracted because you've pumped the cream into Dela's éclair this morning, but might I remind you that us vampires have superior hearing and therefore whispering is a waste of time," Ginny informed me.

I felt my cheeks burn.

"You had the same idea then about an extra pair of hands?" Aria interrupted and nodded at me.

"No, I already used this particular extra set of hands. I've brought him here to feed him and build his strength back up for later," Dela declared.

My cheeks burned even hotter. My hereditary ruddiness was out in full force now.

"So what would you like to eat?" Dela asked me. "Blueberry muffin? Pain au chocolat? Or are you going to be decadent and have a cupcake?"

"Anything but an éclair," I answered, and all three women laughed.

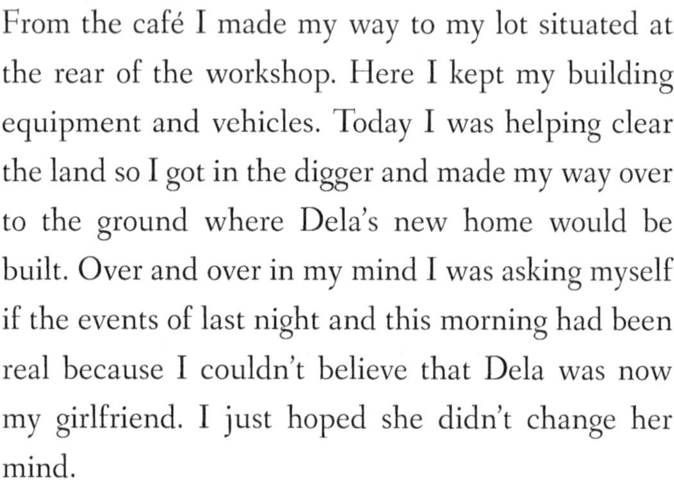

From the café I made my way to my lot situated at the rear of the workshop. Here I kept my building equipment and vehicles. Today I was helping clear the land so I got in the digger and made my way over to the ground where Dela's new home would be built. Over and over in my mind I was asking myself if the events of last night and this morning had been real because I couldn't believe that Dela was now my girlfriend. I just hoped she didn't change her mind.

Zane approached me as I got out of the digger and he gave me instructions as to what they wanted me to do. Vamps weren't happy to do dismantling or digging at speed as they worried what effect it could have on the earth and so that's why they'd brought me in for all the prep work. Gnarly didn't need an earthquake triggering from rapid vampire activity. It was a busy day and by the time I had dropped the digger back off and walked home I was dirty, sweaty, and exhausted.

"Busy day, son?" My dad asked as I walked through the door. He was sitting at the kitchen table looking on his laptop.

"Been clearing Gnarly Wood ready for Dela's house."

In a few days it would be *The Dwelling at Gnarly Wood Nook* thanks to the planning committee.

"And how is your *friendship* with Miss Francis?" He arched a brow.

"Let's put it this way, Father Christmas has brought me my present early this year." I beamed at my dad and he beamed back.

"Well, what a jolly good fellow."

"Thanks, Dad."

"Oh, it was nothing. She just wasn't thinking clearly and needed putting straight, that's all."

"Indeed. So now all we need is for you to confess to Fenella about how you feel about her and both the Anderson men might be loved up for Christmas."

Dad looked at the floor while his cheeks burned. "What nonsense are you spouting now, son? Just because you're loved up doesn't mean I need a woman. Anyway, Fenella doesn't think about me that way. She's too busy for all that relationship nonsense."

"Did she say that?" I couldn't see it with how she looked at my dad.

"Yeah. When her fella left her and she started

organising things for Gnarly. I asked her if she'd ever date again and she spoke of the curse and said she was too busy anyway and that her ex had put her off for life."

"When was the last time she said that?"

"Er, it was a while back, but she'd said it many times and she's not said anything about dating to me since helping out here. Just said she was glad to have something to occupy her time, and that she enjoyed spending time with me because we'd known each other a long time and understood each other. She asked me if I fancied a nice, home-cooked meal at her house in the new year once all the main festivities were out of the way. I said I'd look forward to it."

"You're so dumb, Dad. You've agreed to a date." I laughed.

"No no no, no no no," he said, and then his brow furrowed, and he stroked a hand down his beard. "Oh jingle bells, is it a date?"

I laughed harder.

"Never mind you laughing at your old man. I've not dated in years and what if it isn't? What if Fen doesn't think about me that way at all?"

I tapped the side of my nose. "Believe in Christmas miracles, Dad," I said, repeating his words of yesterday back to him.

"Anyway, never mind my love life, what happened yesterday when you went to see your mother?"

I told him about how she'd not been interested.

"I'm sorry, lad. You deserve better."

"I know I do, but do you know what? I'm glad I went and found out for myself what she was like because now I feel I can draw a line under the whole thing. You have been a brilliant single dad, and Fen stepped up like an auntie when you couldn't be around. I think I turned out okay." I smiled at my father.

"You turned out more than okay, and one day you'll take over the mantle of Santa and you'll do all your ancestors proud," he said, wiping a tear from his eye.

"Let's make this Christmas a good one for the Andersons too," I said.

Dad nodded. "Let's do that."

I went in to hug him and he swerved me. "Don't think so, lad. You seen and smelled the state of you? Get in the damn shower, boy, before Miss Francis comes back round to dirty you all up again."

～ CHAPTER ～
NINETEEN

Dela

Aria was amazing at running the bookshop. Customers had flocked in being nosy about the new building, and she'd drawn them over to her side of the store by coming around the tables with small pamphlets with book samples in and some bookmarks with quotes from the books we had in stock. She'd arranged all of the deliveries and chosen the books. I'd not had to do a thing. When I'd brought up the subject of financing the bookstore, she said she'd taken care of it for now but would discuss it further with Callie when she returned.

I double-checked that she wasn't using her vamp powers to enthral people into purchasing, but she reminded me that the majority of Gnarly were immune due to protection spells. I was used to handling the food side of things and the new kitchen equipment actually made things a little easier once I'd worked out what made what. It hadn't taken long to get the first batch of fresh cupcakes ready, and we'd cheated slightly on this first morning. Aria had popped to a bakery in London and whizzed back with their pastries, as otherwise I'd have been baking half the night.

And that would have meant no doing of all the lovely things with Nick all night long.

"Oh God, look at your face," Ginny whined. "It's enough to make me puke. Just a few days ago at the wedding you were like me, single and ready to mingle, and now you've gone to the dark side."

"Sorry." I shrugged and then I smiled again.

"Yeah, you look really sorry. But it's fine. One day soon I will find a rich man who adores me and who I can face sleeping with until they die."

"Nooooo, Ginny. You need to find your 'one'," I insisted. "Don't you believe in true love?"

"I know love exists because I've seen people fall in love enough times, but it's not for me. Unless of course I fall in love with a rich man and then he's either already a vampire or he lets me turn him, but then what if I get bored? Aria gets bored with Bernard."

"I love my husband," Aria protested. "However, yes, sometimes I find him very tiresome. My working here shall be good for the both of us. And it's pronounced Bairrnarrd," she added.

Ginny looked at me and rolled her eyes.

Once I'd convinced myself Ginny would stay pleasant with the bakery customers and not run a credit check on all the male customers, I took myself off into the kitchens to do a ton of batch cooking. Callie had secured a week's leave for the both of us while she enjoyed her honeymoon, stating we'd not had a break in forever, so I'd not had to worry about baking anything to send to the *Sugar Shack* AKA Tooth Fairy HQ. I felt guilty then because I knew I'd been putting on my sister. More often than not she'd baked extra and sent them to headquarters saying they were my contribution and yet I'd accepted my payment like I was owed it. It was time I grew up and become the responsible adult I knew I could be, and seeing as my new home was going to have a spanking new kitchen...

By the time the day drew to a close, I'd had so much fun working in the café with Aria and Ginny that I decided I would start to work there properly. Part-time, but I would help my sister so that her and Lawrie could have some time as a couple, and I would start baking at home so that Callie no longer had to be responsible for my Tooth Fairy work.

And then like I'd wished her here, my sister and Lawrie suddenly appeared in the middle of the store.

"What in the absolute fuck has happened here? Where's my cupcake café?" she yelled at me.

We'd closed the shop and Ginny took Aria and Lawrie with her for a drink at the Vampire's In(n) so that they could update Lawrie on the café update. That left me with my sister, who stood with her hands on her hips looking at me like she had the time I'd snuck back through my bedroom window aged fourteen drunk and with a hickey and she'd had to sneak me black coffee and use her best concealer to stop me from getting grounded.

"So would you like to tell me how I left you looking after my cupcake café and I've come back and the building is entirely changed? Did you sell it to a wizard while I was away? I've only been gone for five days."

"I would tell you, but I think instead I will have someone else explain it to you. The person who is responsible," I replied, happy to hand this shitshow over to its deserved recipient—Mya.

I called her. "I need you at the café *urgently*."

Mya appeared within the minute and took one look at my sister's face and grabbed her. "Wayne, leave this innocent body and come face your interview with me at the house."

"What are you talking about, Mya? Who the hell is Wayne? What have you done to my café?" Callie shouted.

Mya winced. "I have superior hearing. Your yelling is painful."

"Arrrrrrrrgggghhhhhh," Callie screamed. "Someone answer me. Right. NOW."

Mya shook her head at my sister's dramatic response. "Sweetie, this is your wedding present from Death and me. Well, I say the both of us because that is the couple thing to do, but really it was all me. What do you think?" She gestured around the place with her right hand.

Callie slowly turned and looked around the new interior. "Th-this is mine? No one sold it?"

"It's yours. Don't you remember our conversation just last week when you said if you weren't going to die, you'd extend the place and convert it to Books and Buns? Well, I got it done with a lot of help from our friends."

"And the upstairs has also been extended," I added. "You have a brand-new home for you and your new husband. I made sure you got a king-sized bed and a soundproofed room with blackout blinds for if Lawrie wants to sleep undisturbed."

Callie slowly walked around the café and bookstore, her hands running over the elaborate shelving Merrin had erected. "It's just beautiful, beyond my wildest dreams, and that's why I thought you'd sold my building. I didn't think this could possibly be mine, and after last week when I'd thought I was going to die... now I find I'm not only happily married but I own the best business in the universe." She flung her arms around Mya, who hugged her tightly.

"You're so welcome, bestie," Mya said. "And you also have some help. Aria is happily running the bookstore side if that's okay with you?"

Callie held Mya at arms-length. "You spoke with Aria amicably?"

"To be honest, I'm more jealous she gets to run the bookstore than about her having dated my man in the past. Plus, I'm stronger than her, so if she makes a move near Death, she'll have made a move to her absolute final undead death."

"Now I know I'm home and not hallucinating because that is the most Mya thing I ever heard," Callie said to me. "Right, are you going to get me a coffee and a cupcake for me to enjoy in my new place or what?" She then turned back to Mya. "And who the hell is Wayne?"

We got Callie caught up on all things *Books and Buns* and then she regaled us with tales of the many places her and Lawrie had visited in the past four days.

"But after we'd been around the Christmas markets in Berlin, I just wanted to come home. Christmas in Gnarly is so magical and this time it would be my first as a married woman. So I told Lawrie and here we are. Back a few days early and now I find I have an entirely new home to settle into."

"Your tree is in the new living room," I told her. "But you have space for a lot more decorations now."

Lawrie re-appeared and started to look around the shop. "So what do you think, wife? Are you happy, or am I to have strong words with my daughter about running things past her father first?" He gave Mya a dirty look to which she just stuck out her tongue.

"I think it's fabulous. Now shall we go see what our new home above is like?"

"Oh I think we should," Lawrie said, his eyes darkening with lust.

"And that's me leaving." I turned to my sister. "I've other things to catch you up on, so I'll see you here in the morning, okay?"

"Sure." Callie gave me a large hug, did the same to Mya and then we left the newlyweds to it.

And I went straight to Nick's because I might not be newly wedded, but I was newly bedded.

Dela

Early the next morning, I was back at the café. Callie was chatting with Aria, and I could see her excitement and enthusiasm in her unrestrained smiles and the way she kept spinning around taking everything in. She waved as she saw me.

"You, lady. Aria has told me about you and Nick. I need alllll the details. You have been busy while I've been away."

Huh, she didn't know the half of it.

"I may have a boyfriend now," I said dismissively, but with a smirk upon my lips, as I went into the back to grab my apron and hair net. We'd not changed those, so they were still bright pink. Callie followed me in.

"What happened to not dating people in Gnarly?"

"Stan Anderson happened," I answered, walking back out to the counter where Callie followed me again. Naturally she then forced me to tell her everything while Aria also listened in from the other side of the shop.

"Oh, I am so happy that we are both in love." Callie was practically bouncing on her feet. "It would have made me feel guilty to be so happy when you were single."

"Steady on. I've only been dating the guy for a couple of days," I said. "I think the 'L' word is a bit premature."

"You look loved up. It's coming. I see it in your eyes. Your brain just needs to catch up," she said.

I looked over at Aria who was desperately trying not to laugh, and I mouthed, "Help."

"She's a newlywed. I've been there. Don't worry it wears off. Now, are we going to open up? It's almost nine and people are already outside."

"Where is Lawrie, anyway?" I asked my sister.

"I've sent him out to get some new Christmas decorations from London. Ones that will last a long time in order to satisfy Gnarly's eco-policies of reusing things."

"That won't last either," said Aria. "Being able to order him around. Newlywed males would basically get down on all fours and pretend to be your pet dog knowing that later you'll do whatever they like in the bedroom."

"Yeah, well while it's happening, I'll make the most of it, and in return I'll do doggy in the bedroom."

I fake retched and went to open up to stop my sister from saying anymore. I was so happy in my new relationship with Nick, but Callie's enthusiasm was threatening to be every bit as in your face as her previous pink café.

We'd agreed to walk over to the wood after work, so I could see the first day's progress and show my sister where my house was going to be. The café had been extremely busy as villagers came in to not only experience the new café but to congratulate my sister and tell her how beautiful she'd looked, given they'd watched the wedding in the boulevard. Many had brought her gifts. Lawrie had dropped off Christmas decorations for the bookstore and café and so we'd also decorated the place in between serving and cleaning. Some of the villagers we knew well had joined in with getting the place looking festive and I'd rigged up my iPhone to play Christmas music into the store. The spirit of Christmas was truly kicking in and I felt a fresh sense of excitement watching my sister get her business and home ready, knowing that my own place would be finished tomorrow. *I also need decorations!* I realised. Tomorrow I would go into London myself to get some.

For as much as Callie and I had shared Christmases in the flat over the past five years, they'd come with the ghosts of Christmases past, and the fact that with our adoptive parents we'd celebrated the birth of Christ in Church and received no more than a Christingle orange. This year, I realised I was not only focused on the present but also on the future. I could feel things changing inside of me for the better, because in my stomach there was now hope and excitement instead of bitter resentment.

"I bloody love the store," Callie said as we set off towards the park. The air was crisp and we took in the decorated boulevard with its white twinkling lights and the huge tree.

"Yes, I've noticed," I replied, before giggling.

'Oh shut up," she said, pushing me in the arm.

"You look much happier too, Dela. There's just a different air about you. Whether it's Nick, or the house..."

"I think it's both," I confessed as we carried on strolling. "I have a new, exciting relationship and I'm finally putting down firm roots on my own. I was in two minds about the house at first because it's future proofed, built for a family, and I wasn't anywhere near that position, so it raised a lot of issues for me. But now, even if things with Nick don't work out, I know I'm going to make the place mine, my home, for now. Like I'm going to buy a light-up reindeer for outside!"

It was Callie's turn to laugh.

"God, what is happening to us both? We're happy. Blissfully happy. I can't help but wait for something to go wrong. I know I shouldn't think like that, but it is only six days since I almost died."

"Hmm, well, there is something I need to talk to you about." I wet my lips, feeling the nerves kick in.

Callie sighed in resignation. "I knew it was all too good to be true. Go on."

I stopped walking and fidgeted a little, pulling down the sleeves of my coat. "I met up with Sheridan on Wednesday to ask her about our fae parents. She came here to talk to me as she wanted to know what suddenly had me searching for information. We did this, walked to where my home was going to be built, and she told me that we'd both been born in the exact spot where my house will be."

"What? That's crazy. What are the chances of that?"

"I know. Anyway, when Sheridan saw it, she broke down, and confessed that..." I swallowed.

"She's our mother," Callie finished.

"*Yes*. How did you know what I was going to say?"

Callie sighed. "When we first met her, I just had this feeling. I can't explain it, but Sheridan was so kind in getting us set up in Gnarly, and the allowance we received seemed entirely too generous for providing treats to the *Sugar Shack*. When she left us to it... there was a point where she seemed to want to say something else. At the time I did wonder if she wanted to tell us more about our parents, but when she didn't, I just told myself I was reading more into it than was there. That if she'd been our mother, she'd have told us. When you just said she broke down, I knew what you were going to say next."

"And what do you think about that? That she's our mother?"

"I can't help but wonder why she didn't welcome us as her daughters when we met her in London," she replied quietly.

While we walked the rest of the way to the development, I filled her in on the story as far as I knew it.

"She couldn't utter another word after she saw where my home was being built. It was hard, but I let her go. She more or less ran out of Gnarly, but I didn't take it personally. From her face when she'd collapsed, I could see it had brought it all back. Her lost love and the children she'd had to give up."

"I don't know what I think about all this. It's so much to take in," Callie said, bringing a shaky hand up to her forehead.

"That's the other reason I let her go. I also needed time to think about things."

"And what conclusion did you reach?"

"I want to know the rest of it. I want to ask her about our father and if she's in touch with him at all, and I want to get to know Sheridan better. She is our mother, and even if she never becomes more than the person who settled us in Gnarly, I want to meet up with her regularly." I searched my sister's face trying to see what she was thinking.

"I can't promise anything, but I will come with you to see her and find out more. Now the ball has begun rolling, I think we might as well know everything."

I rocked on my heels. "So, about that. I'm going to go Christmas shopping into the centre of London tomorrow and…"

"You thought you might see if you could meet up with Sheridan while you were there?"

I nodded.

"She's probably busy. It is Christmas Eve tomorrow, you know?"

"I know, but it doesn't hurt to ask, does it?"

"I guess not. The café is closing at lunch time tomorrow, so I'll see if Ginny will come to cover my morning shift."

"Great. Hey, if nothing else, we can have some fun Christmas shopping."

"Fun? In the centre of London on Christmas Eve with all the panic buyers. You're insane." She shook her head at me.

Then we both came to the clearing and gazed at the beginnings of my house. The bottom part was almost built. It took my breath away, watching as the vampires worked at a crazy speed, the building going up in front of my eyes.

Zane spotted us and came walking towards me. "Dela, what do you think so far?"

His answer came when I burst into tears. The building already looked incredible and the lights they had up so they could work in the dark lit it up with warm tones and made it look so homely.

"Oh, shit. I didn't mean to upset you."

"She's overcome, that's all," Callie said. "The place looks amazing. I'm incredibly jealous."

As my sister said she was jealous of me, for the first time ever that I could remember, I realised that it no longer made a jot of difference to me who did what first. I wanted us both to be happy, and out of the two of us, my sister's happiness would always come before my own.

"D-do you want to live there, with Lawrie? I w-would let you have it."

"Oh, Dela." She flung her arms around me. "You are the best sister in the world, but I have my new home above my amazing shop, and this... this is where you put down your roots and create your family. I'm totally down for a girly night though. I can picture us snuggling under blankets watching the snow come down outside of the windows while an open fire crackles.

"Yeah, wooden structure, so fake fire," I said. "But yes to all the other stuff." Stepping out of my sister's embrace, I hugged and thanked Zane and then went around and thanked all the other people who were working on my house and who would be there on Christmas Eve in order to finish my gorgeous new home. And though I knew on Christmas Day a lot of things would still be missing in terms of furniture because the place wouldn't be finished until later on Christmas Eve and the stores would be closed then, I figured as long as I got my bed and current belongings in place, I would be fine —even if my lunch was a turkey toasted sandwich purchased from Costa tomorrow.

Callie and I walked back to Gnarly chatting about all the exciting times ahead and what shops we'd try to head for tomorrow and then I made my way to Nick's.

He wrapped me in his arms and kissed me deeply. "I missed you all day," he said.

"I missed you all day too," I confessed.

"Fenella wants you to know that if you get bored on Christmas Day, you are to make your way over to hers because she always has extra food," he said.

"Tell her thank you. In fact, I need to pop to the laundrette actually, so I'll tell her myself. You okay if I pop back to the twins' place to pick up my laundry? I'll come back as soon as I can."

"I'll drive you; it'll be quicker. Then I'll come back here while you sort your laundry. I can be making us some dinner."

"Perfect. I'll provide dessert."

"I hope it's you and a can of whipped cream."

"Wait and see." I winked.

Nick locked the door behind him, and we walked around to get in his car, then headed to the twins' house to collect up my dirty laundry.

"We would have sent out a search party, but Jason told us that you and Nick were doing the horizontal tango," they said as I walked into the living room to say hi.

I gave a slow nod as I acknowledged them both. "I'm so sorry. I know it feels like I've ditched you both, but between Nick, and the new house, and some family stuff, and the new shop, I've been running around like a headless chicken."

"It's fine. We understand. Our shop has been busy and then we have been practising being separate with Jason. He is helping us," Milly said.

"Oh yeah, how?"

"He came into the store, and we were explaining how we wanted to be doing things separately. He was so understanding," Tilly said. "He said men would be fine with us being together or separate, that it would be fine either way. And then yesterday he took me to the bistro and the day before he took Milly to the pizzeria. He's invited us both to a hotel tonight to show us how it's okay for us to be together."

"NO," I yelled. "Absolutely not." I then told them what Jason would be expecting. The twins both froze in place.

"Milly. Tilly. You haven't both turned back into dolls, have you?"

Milly blinked. "I cannot believe Jason would expect us to do such a thing. I thought he was a nice man."

"He is, largely," I said, and then I explained how a lot of male brains worked and that the twins would have served up quite the fantasy in Jason's mind.

"Well tonight he will have the fantasy of having paid for a hotel and no one going to it," Tilly said. "This is why we must date separately, Milly."

"I agree. Now what shall we do tonight now we are not going to a hotel for date training?"

"Shall we watch *The Holiday*?" they said at the same time, both nodding at the other in agreement.

"Have a lovely evening then and I'll see you tomorrow sometime, okay? I need to give you your presents," I said. I'd not even bought anyone anything yet. It was another reminder of how self-absorbed I could be. These girls had been true friends to me, giving me a place to stay, and what had I done in return? Spent the last few days ignoring them. It wasn't good enough. I collected my laundry and went back to the car.

"You were a while."

"Yes, well, I just saved the twins from an experience I'd rather not think of."

"Oh yeah?"

I told him about Jason.

"Oh my god. Well, that has just given me quite the idea. While you're doing your laundry, I think I'll rope Merrin in to give Jason quite the surprise."

"Merrin? Isn't he a gloomy, miserable being?"

"Merrin can be a right laugh when you get to know him."

"Oh, well, I want all the details when I get back."

"Can you call the twins for me and ask what room number he's in before you go?"

"Sure."

I spoke to the twins and then Nick dropped me off near to the laundrette and I kissed him and said I'd see him later.

Walking the rest of the way to the laundrette, I began singing Mariah's *All I Want for Christmas is You*. The next thing I heard was an angry spit from a cat as it launched at me, knocking my laundry from my hands. Then I felt a pop in my ear.

Nick

The chance to have a laugh at Jason's expense was like being given your dream Christmas gift, second to getting my new girlfriend of course. I called Merrin and filled him in on what Jason had done.

"Sometimes our friend leaves me speechless," Merrin replied.

I didn't mention that sometimes Merrin went into large bouts of silence or slowness where his undead state became extremely obvious and therefore he was speechless on many an occasion.

"I'll pick you up in half an hour. First I need to ask his mum if she'll let me borrow two costumes from the community centre's fancy-dress cupboard."

"Come whenever you're ready. I have no plans

and I'm trying to sort out my land. My projects are piling up."

"Okay. See you later."

I called Fenella.

"Hello, sweetheart. I can see your girlfriend in the doorway. Are you wanting to talk to her?"

"No, it's you I want to talk to. Dela's getting some laundry done, very last minute."

"Hmm, is that because she's been distracted of late by a certain young man?"

"Maybe, but I think largely it's just Dela. Anyhow, I need to ask you a favour…"

When I let her in on what her son had been up to, Fenella told me to collect whatever I needed.

"Security will be on the door at the community centre. I'll ring ahead and let them know you're coming and then the keypad number is 2820. Remember it as an owl. Two-weight, Two-woh."

"Gotcha. Thanks, Fen."

"No. Thank you, Nick, for giving my son lessons on what's acceptable behaviour. If he wants a threesome, that's his business, but not with those two girls who don't understand life properly. I doubt very much he'd have got anywhere once they realised his intentions anyway."

I ended the call and made my way first to the community centre and then to Merrin's.

As I pulled up at his place it became apparent that the stuff he collected had got out of hand. There was barely a piece of ground to be seen. A lot of Gnarly's recyclable stuff came Merrin's way and it seemed too much stuff had landed here. I resolved after the new year to come give him a hand in organising it all and maybe in helping him learn to say no. But right now, it was time to have fun.

Merrin and I had changed at his place and then climbed into my car. I'd just pulled into the hotel car park, which was a short drive away from Gnarly in St Albans.

I'd wanted us to dress up as Milly and Tilly, but the nearest costumes I'd been able to get were those of the girls from Abba.

It meant though that the hotel porters and receptionists just figured we were there for a festive fancy-dress party as we walked through and said hi and didn't bat an eyelid.

After going up in the lift to the third floor, I indicated for Merrin to wait outside the lifts while I called the twins, having got their number from Dela after she'd spoken to them.

"Tilly speaking."

"Tilly. I'm here. Can you phone Jason and ask him to get into bed naked and turn the lights out?"

She giggled. "I will. What a shame it will be dark and you aren't able to record his misfortune."

"True, but I will tell you all about it, in detail," I replied.

"Thank you, Nick. I will ring him now," she said.

"Pretend you're outside his door," I added.

"Will do."

Merrin and I made our way to Jason's room, and I put my ear to the door. I could vaguely hear him talking, but not the actual words. We jumped as we heard the door unlock, but thankfully Jason didn't open it.

"Ready?" I said to Merrin.

"Let's Lay All Your Love on Jason," Merrin replied, to which I looked at him strangely.

"It's an Abba song," he sighed. "*Lay All Your Love On Me.*"

"Oh. Good one."

I pushed open the door. We could just make out the shape of Jason in the bed.

"Hey, girls," Jason said, his voice wavering. "I have to say I was just expecting for us to chat about you considering dating one man. This is really, well, unexpected, but I am here for it."

I crawled in at one side of the bed and Merrin crawled in at the other like we'd discussed.

"Oh, you're both cold, and dressed. But I'm happy to warm you both up. How will this work though? Who do I warm up first? This is a new one on me too. I just want to let you know that. It's actually, well, a first for me altogether to be honest."

I froze. Jason was forever telling me about his latest conquests, the utter lying toad.

Then Merrin spoke, revealing a hidden talent. He perfectly mimicked the twins' voices.

"Well, as you know we are new to this too, so we can all learn together. So to start with, maybe you could feel my breast over the top of my clothes?"

"O-okay then. I c-can do that."

I detected movement and a rustle of clothing.

"Oh yeah," Merrin said, though I knew Jason was feeling a rolled-up sock.

"Now, touch me here," Merrin said, and I waited.

"What the fuck?" yelled Jason loudly, leaning over me to switch the light on. He saw us in our Abba suits and jumped out of bed swearing and calling us all the names under the sun, but we were doubled over.

"I had your dick in my hand, man. Okay it was

covered in your flares, but still. Oh my god, I thought the girls were men. I'm traumatized," he said. But he was wasting his breath because Merrin and I couldn't stop laughing.

My phone rang and I wiped the tears from my eyes to answer the phone to Fenella.

"Hey, Fen." A bubble of mirth left my mouth.

"I'm sorry to interrupt but Dela is acting very strangely."

I stopped laughing and stood up. "What do you mean?"

"I'd left her to it as I was busy around the back. I came out about ten minutes ago and she was muttering to herself. I asked if she was okay, and she told me to mind my own business. Her eyes flashed red when she said it. I think that demon's inside her, Nick."

"Stay safe. We'll be right there," I said. Then I turned to my friends. "I need you two to come with me to the launderette. Dela's in danger."

The journey to the laundrette seemed to take forever. Jason had quickly got dressed and checked out. Merrin and I had taken off our wigs and thrown them in the back of my car, but we remained in the Abba suits. It was the least of my worries. Merrin dropped me off outside the launderette but I asked him and Jason to stay outside. I didn't want them being possesssed. They weren't protected.

Mya stepped out from around the corner. I'd called her but told her straight that she was to do nothing until I got there unless Dela got into difficulties in the meantime.

"Do you have that sphere ready this time?" I asked her.

"Yes."

"Okay, let's go."

I pushed open the door of the laundrette.

"Oooh, it's you," Dela said, her eyes flashing red.

Then for a moment she became Dela again. As I heard her say, "What the hell?" I felt a prodding at my ear, but then Dela held her own ear and her eyes flashed again.

"You did something. I can't enter you."

Wayne/Dela went into her bag and pulled out a piece of paper and unfolded it. "Do you know what I have here? I have your brother's phone number, Nick. Dela was going to ring it you know? She preferred him to you. I might just give him a ring now and ruin your Christmas. I could sleep with him, and you couldn't do a damn thing. Might be fun to try out what it's like from a woman's point of view. I'm only used to that frigid bitch of a wife I had. Never bloody satisfied in any area, that one."

"What is your problem?" Mya asked. "You came to the Home of Wayward Souls because the jury was out on whether you were good or evil, but since you escaped you've only shown a nasty side."

Wayne/Dela grimaced. "I hate Christmas. Everyone being so bloody happy. That bitch left me at the beginning of December. She said she'd decided to leave me and go back to where she was brought up. That she was taking the kids. I found out she'd been living a double life the whole time I'd known her. I didn't give a damn about her, but I had plans for Christmas, for being there with my own kids, and she ruined it all. So when she came back to the house to pick up the last of her and the kids' belongings, I decided to show her how she'd ruined my Christmas. While she was in the bathroom, I set the decorations on fire. I didn't realise the fumes were toxic..."

"And she made it, but you didn't?" Mya said.

"Yeah and now she has everything because she's rid of me, so she got the perfect Christmas after all."

"You think so, do you?" Mya placed her hands

over her chest. "Only I've checked out what's happening. Your wife now has two children who are distraught because their father died. So I think we can safely say that they aren't having a good Christmas and you got your wish in ruining it after all."

"Fuck." Wayne/Dela dropped to their knees.

"Now the reason you're stuck is because it crossed your mind while you were there setting the fire that if you locked her in the house and went out, you'd get the insurance money and the kids. Unfortunately, the smoke inhalation got to you before you could think any further. So I have to decide what I think you would have done."

"I hated her for what she did, but I wouldn't have taken my kids' mum away. I just wanted to show her how she'd ruined Christmas for me. I was angry."

"And why are you in Gnarly now? You can only escape the Home of the Wayward if there's a resolution to be found here in Gnarly village itself. What's tying you to this place?" Mya asked him.

"My wife is here," he said. "But I can't get to her. She's put an enchantment on the house she's staying at. Stupid witch."

"She's here? In Gnarly?" Mya asked.

"Yes, her dad was only too happy for her to come here. He never liked me."

I had a sneaking suspicion I knew who his wife was.

"Is her name Alicia?" I asked Wayne/Dela.

His head shot up towards me. "Yes. And don't think I hadn't noticed how she watched you. Didn't take her long to move on, did it? So I figured if I could possess you I'd be able to get to her, have a way of being a family again, but then *she* showed up." He pointed to Mya. "So I possessed the cat and waited. But I seem to have missed you getting protection from the bitch. No doubt because the cat slept most of the bloody day."

"It's time for you to leave this body now, Wayne, and come into this sphere." Mya whirled the red and gold sphere above her hand.

"Not until I've seen my wife," he demanded.

"Can't you force him out?" I asked Mya. "You're the queen."

"Not until his journey is complete and I guess right now it's not." She turned to him. "I'm going to get your wife. Behave yourself."

Mya was only gone for a moment, returning with a shaken looking Alicia.

"Hello, darling. Miss me?" he asked, his mouth forming a slit of a grimace afterward.

"How am I supposed to take you seriously when you're in the body of a fae woman?" she scoffed.

His eyes narrowed. "I've never been enough for you, have I? Not even enough for you to tell me that you were a witch. Doing Zumba my arse. You were at coven meetings weren't you? Dancing naked around bonfires and having orgies."

"And that's why I didn't tell you. Because you're an idiot. I only stayed with you because of the children. Why it took me so long to realise I married a moron is beyond me. And now look at you. Even in death you're pathetic. You possessed a fae? What's your next move? A dance in the woodland?"

I watched Mya who remained with the sphere above her hand, waiting. Alicia was the same, standing waiting for his reply. She turned to me. "I guess we'll not be meeting up in the new year now?"

The next moment there was a small fae woman on the ground and the sphere in Mya's hand expanded with a pop for a brief moment, turning red.

"That's me going back to Gnarly with this one. He's definitely going to hell for all the trouble he's caused," she said and disappeared.

Meanwhile Dela returned to her normal size.

"Dela! Are you okay?" I helped her up off the floor.

"Yes, I'm fine. Well, I will be now I know he's gone and won't be taking over me again. We all need protection spells to prevent this happening again though." She looked at Alicia.

"Chantelle can do them all." Alicia nodded.

"But how did you manage to get the spirit out?" I asked her. "Did you just figure going small meant he'd be ejected?"

"Eventually. First *she*." She pointed at Alicia. "Pissed me off because she was derogatory about the powers of the fae, and *then*, she said you'd not be meeting up in the new year and she damn well got that straight." She walked up to Alicia. "Because he's my boyfriend now."

Alicia stepped back. "I think I'm going to have a rest from dating anyway. Just focus on my children for a while."

"So you ejected the spirit because you got jealous?" I laughed.

"Yup. I thought how can I get this pissy bastard out of me so I can go claim my man, and that was the way. I did it, I made myself a small fae."

She did it three more times. "Okay, I'm tired

now. I think it's time to go back to yours," she told me.

"I agree. It's been a long day. Let's get you in bed resting from your ordeal." We said goodbye to Alicia and to Fenella who came out from the back of the launderette. Once outside I said goodbye and thank you to Merrin and Jason and then we made our way back to mine.

After running Dela a nice hot bath, I helped her get dried off and into bed.

"Do you want a cuppa or a hot toddy or anything?"

"I want you," she said.

"Hmm, whereas I think you need to rest," I protested.

"I think the last person to enter my body was a dick called Wayne, and I'd like that memory replaced with being entered by a dick belonging to my boyfriend," she requested.

"Okay, but once I've rid you of all thoughts of Wayne, you rest," I ordered.

"Fine. But it might take me a while." She winked.

I dived under the covers and gave in to her demands.

CHAPTER TWENTY-TWO

Dela

I stayed wrapped in Nick's arms until the alarm went off. I was off to London with my sister. I saw I had a text from Callie and a few missed calls.

Mya called me this morning. Oh my god. Are you okay? Tried calling but no answer. Ring me ASAP.

I phoned her back from the kitchen.

"I'm fine."

"What the hell happened? I've heard Mya's version, but I want to hear yours."

"Look, let me get ready and we can talk about it on our way in to London."

"You sure you're okay to go?"

"I need to go, and not even because we're going to talk with Sheridan, but because I need to go shopping and do something normal."

"Okay. I'll see you at mine as soon as you're ready. I'll have Lawrie and Mya whizz us to London."

"Okay."

"Jesus. Are you sure you're all right?" Callie was looking me up and down. "And you went total faery. Wow. How was your first time?" She winked and it made me laugh. It was a much-needed laugh. We were walking around Harrods looking at the cute but very expensive Christmas stuff. Later, we intended to go around some Christmas markets, but for now we wanted a warm and a wander around the decadent Christmas displays. Their shop window was amazing with woodland scenes with trees decorated with Swarovski crystals. After the events of last night, I had wondered if I'd feel festive again after experiencing Wayne's hatred of Christmas, but London at Christmas was certainly putting me back in the mood.

"It just happened so naturally," I answered. "I

was trying deep down to get him out of me and then I was small and free. You know my biggest fear was not getting back to human size, but it was easy. I practiced it another twice in the bathroom this morning."

"I did the same when I first did it. I have to say I've not used the ability in years. We don't really have need to in Gnarly, but I guess it's good we can both change, in case we get chance to go to the court."

"I don't want to go there," I confessed.

"You don't?"

"No. My home is Gnarly. I was born in Gnarly. Sheridan can come to Gnarly. If our father can't or won't, I'm not sure I'm willing to go there. What if it compromises our safety and we bring danger back to the fell?"

"Let's see what Sheridan has to say later. But I hear what you're saying."

We visited a café where we enjoyed a Christmas wrap and followed it up with a hot chocolate and then it was time to meet Sheridan at the bar where we'd first met five years before.

When we entered, she was sitting at a table twiddling with her fingers. I saw her brush her hands down her skirt before she gave us a small wave. Her hand shook and I felt sorry for the mother who'd had to carry all this pain for so long. Because that's what she wore on her face— pain—and I just instinctively knew she'd pushed it deep down inside for so long. After being possessed it somehow gave me an inside track on how she must have felt being unable to confess the words she wanted to speak.

We sat down at the table alongside her and I regretted my big lunch and hot chocolate because right now I could have used a glass of wine, but I felt I'd just vomit if I had another thing. After we both refused anything to eat or drink, Sheridan asked for a water.

"I guess you're just wanting to get this over with, so I'll tell you the rest," she said.

"No, we just ate and drank too much already. I can't even look at food right now," I explained.

"Oh, okay. By the way, congratulations, Callie. Did you have a nice honeymoon?"

"It was great, but I was happy to be home for Christmas."

"Is that how you really see Gnarly? As home?"

"Yes. It's why I'm so excited about my new business and apartment, and Dela is almost wetting herself about getting in her new place for Christmas."

"Thanks, sis, for that."

"She dealt with our nappies, did she not? It's not a new visual."

We both looked at Sheridan then because it was true. She had.

"I guess that's a good segue into the rest of our story," Sheridan said, and then she began.

"When they put me in prison, it wasn't like a place where cold-blooded murderers went. It was just a very basic cell, and I had many chores to do throughout the day, including a lot of baking for the Tooth Fairy headquarters. They said I would stay there forever unless one day either of my children sought help from the fae."

"So you were released when we contacted you?"

"Yes, in a way. I was given board and lodgings in the Tooth Fairy Headquarters and recruited as a tooth fairy. Before I'd just been a lower fae and you were half lower fae, half royal blood, but being born out of the courts on human soil meant you were earth fae until that point. When you got in touch, I was instructed to introduce you slowly to fae life via the tooth fairy business and told to make sure you were safe and looked after. In return they would make sure you had enough money and a safe place to live."

"Who did this? Who released you and gave you those instructions?" I asked.

"Your father's wife. The queen," she replied.

For a moment none of us said anything. It was clear to see that our father having a wife caused Sheridan pain.

"Theirs is a good marriage I am told. They seem in love and they have four children: your half-kin. But there are rules in the royal court and unfortunately you two cannot be acknowledged officially and cannot meet your two brothers and two sisters. I am so very sorry."

"We have each other. That is fine. We don't know them and they don't know us," Callie said firmly. "We have no wish to become involved in royal fae business. But what of our father, the king? Does he wish to acknowledge us... unofficially?"

"I requested an audience with Vania yesterday and we met in secret. She said that I can meet with you as often as I like and asked if I wished to move to the fell. It would mean the end of Tooth Fairy business and contact with the royal court for all three of us for good."

"So there will never be any contact with our father?"

"No. There cannot be. You were a product of a

secret forbidden affair and too many fae politics rest upon it. You can never be acknowledged in the courts. That is the price for all of our safety. I am lucky the queen is a kind woman; another would have had me executed."

"But you were in love," I protested.

"We were, but who knows if it would have lasted? I'd like to think so, but I can't know for sure, and he does love Vanya."

"How can you know?"

"I know this sounds crazy, but not only do I feel it within me having spoken to the queen and the other people of the court, but on my way out of Gnarly when I was upset, I bumped into a strange fellow. Tall and gaunt. He grabbed my hand and asked me if I was okay. Then he said that everything would work out, but while there would be upheaval for me, other things must be left in place. That the love was pure."

"Merrin," I said.

"Pardon?" Sheridan questioned.

"The man you met was Merrin. He's an artist. He sometimes has the sight."

"Ah, that makes sense then. When he held my hand, I felt a sense of peace as his words washed over me. He most definitely has a gift."

"And so how do you feel about the queen's proposition?"

"I would move to Gnarly in a heartbeat, but that all depends on whether you girls would want that, and whether you could forgive me for the past."

I pulled my mother to her feet and threw my arms around her, and before I knew it Callie had joined in. Soon we were a mass of sobs and then we made tentative plans for the future.

Part of me felt emotionally exhausted and ready to go back to Gnarly after we said goodbye to our mother, but another part of me fancied mead and the markets. Two meads later, Callie and I shopped up a storm and no fucks were given about buying new things, because we both were having fresh starts, the decorations would be used every year, and wasn't it the season to be jolly?

Whizzed back to Gnarly with our belongings, I went to Nick's. He took one look at all the shopping I'd done and his face saddened.

"What's the matter?"

"They didn't manage to get your home finished on time, Dela. I'm so sorry, but you'll not be able to spend Christmas there. The vamps are on holiday now and so won't be able to work on it again until the 27th."

I felt my shoulders slump for a moment and then I shrugged them. "Oh well. Fenella said I could go to hers, didn't she? Please let her know that there will be one more for dinner, and my decs will save for next year, so it is what it is. What's important is that I get to spend it with you." I reached up and pulled Nick's head down and kissed him firmly on the lips. "Now take me back to bed, because I'll be blissfully happy as long as I wake up in your arms. I've already got my Christmas presents: you, my mum, and a new house on the way. Plus, I know Santa. I mean, does it really get any better?"

I would find out that because of my boyfriend being a sneaky fucker, it did.

CHAPTER TWENTY-THREE

Dela

I woke and Nick wanted to give me my Christmas present. However, I was horny and so I insisted on giving him his first. I had bought him a few other things, including a new tool belt, and some figure-hugging t-shirts which were a bit of a present for my own eyes too.

Finally, I got up and ready because Nick annoyingly insisted that my present was outside when I'd fancied a morning eating mince pies in my pyjamas.

No sooner did I step out of the door than Mya appeared with Death. I let out a squeal as Mya grabbed me until I found myself standing outside my home. My fully built home. My mouth fell open and I touched my fingertips to my newly parted lips.

"How? You said it wasn't..." I trailed off, now

rendered speechless as I looked at the glorious wooden structure, surrounded by woodland, and lit up by Victorian style lamp standards around the front. Death and Mya said bye and quickly disappeared again.

"I wanted to wrap a huge bow around it, but the twins wouldn't let me, saying it was wasteful," Nick said. "So the one you can see is one Chantelle spelled on it and as soon as we walk through the front door it will disappear."

"It looks amazing. You are such a lying toad, Nick Anderson, telling me my house wasn't finished."

"I know, but my dad said your past Christmases had kind of sucked and so I felt I needed to do all I could to make sure this one didn't."

"And it's completely finished?"

"It is. And though you can't get it furnished yet, at least you can see your home fully built."

I squeezed his hand. "Let's go inside."

As we did the bow disappeared, revealing a Christmas wreath made of holly, mistletoe, and ribbon that hung on the impressive carved front door. The front door looked every bit like a faery door only human sized.

"Merrin designed it," Nick explained.

"I'll have to thank him when I see him because it's incredible," I said, pushing open the front door and walking into my new hallway. The large windows let in vast amounts of light, and I saw the white tiled floor had been the right choice to complete the look. When I had a chance I would get a large plant for the corner of the space.

"Shall we inspect the living room first?' Nick suggested, heading in that direction. I followed him and then he stood back. "After you," he said.

I pushed open the door.

"Merry Christmas," a crowd of family and friends yelled. I looked around me in astonishment as the room was fully furnished and a large tree was in situ in the living room. Among the decorations were all my purchases from London the day before. The furniture was incredible. There were sideboards, coffee tables, and chairs carved from beautiful wood and a dark emerald-green coloured sumptuous sofa. Lights gave out an ambient, amber coloured, warm glow. I couldn't have chosen better myself. I loved it all. The twins came over and hugged me. "Nick asked Merrin to accompany him to our shop to see if he could sense out the things you wanted."

"I hope I chose okay," Merrin said stepping forward.

"You did incredible. Thank you," I said, giving him a hug. He froze in my embrace at first before relaxing. Clearly, he wasn't used to women throwing themselves at him.

I had a look at who else stood around. Mya and Death had only whizzed themselves inside. My sister stood with Lawrie and our mother. Chantelle and the twins stood together at the opposite side of the room from Jason and Fenella.

I realised I could smell cooking. I think the shock had stopped all my bodily functions for a moment.

"I brought Christmas here," Fenella explained, after meeting my gaze. "Now come on girls, and you, Jason. Help me in the kitchen. We'll give my son all the worst jobs."

"I've said I'm sorry four zillion times. I wasn't even trying to do what you think I was," Jason whined.

"No, you were just hoping it would happen anyway," Nick said before laughing.

Jason gave him a dirty look and then followed his mum into the kitchen.

After hugging and thanking everyone, I walked around the rest of my home with Nick. Everything was better than I'd envisaged. I had a home. This was all mine. Upstairs, I took in the huge bed with its beautiful headboard that had carved on it:

Where Faerie folk may rest and sleep until their night is spent.

"Just a moment while I read you this note," Nick said, getting a piece of paper from his pocket and opening it. "Merrin said to tell you that the quote is part of a poem called 'A Faery Song' by Elizabeth T. Dillingham."

"This is beyond my wildest dreams. I cannot wait to move in here. And I'll be able to cook you a meal," I told Nick.

"Sounds good to me. A wench who can satisfy all my appetites," he said, 'oofing' when I elbowed him in the side.

We sat around the most amazing, large oak dining table while Michael Bublé sang Christmas songs in the background. It had twisty legs which reminded me so much of the trees that surrounded us in

Gnarly. Merrin assured us all that it was very sturdy and when he did, Nick and I exchanged a look that left no doubt about what we might be doing on it later.

After a sumptuous feast of all the usual Christmas fayre: pigs in blankets, turkey, roast potatoes, cranberry sauce, sprouts etc, crackers were pulled, and festive hats placed on heads. We groaned at Christmas cracker jokes and people kept snapping photos on their phones, including me. I wanted to remember this Christmas forever.

Sheridan seemed happy as she sat among us. We'd introduced her as our mother, but I didn't know when or if I ever would call her mum. It was too early for that. I was glad she was here to spend Christmas, but there was plenty of time to decide on whether she came to live in Gnarly or not.

"Oh my goodness, I think it's snowing," Chantelle gasped and we all turned to look out of the large window. For a minute there was nothing and I thought she'd imagined it, but then sure enough a flurry of flakes started and then it picked up pace.

And then Santa himself burst through the door.

"Ho ho ho. Merry Christmas," he said to all. "Did I miss dinner?"

Fenella's mouth had dropped open. "What are

you doing here? You never make Christmas dinner. You're too busy."

"I'm delivering a present here, so I can't stay long, but this is on my route," he said.

"So who's the present for?" she asked.

"It's for you. Your son overheard you on the telephone when you apparently said, 'I give up all hope of Stan ever realising I'm in love with him' and he told me last night."

Jason grinned. "I went there after all the dramatics".

"Jason Gardon, you had no right interfering like that. I'm sorry, Stan, I am so embarrassed."

"I'm not." Stan walked over to Fenella and pulled a piece of Mistletoe from his pocket. He held it above her head and swept in to kiss her. Fenella fell into his arms and everyone whooped and cheered.

"I really did see Mummy kissing Santa Claus," Jason said, causing a fresh round of laughter.

"Okay, I'd love to stay longer but my kiss is delivered and in that kiss is my present to you, Fenella. I have loved you for years, so I vow to not waste any more of them. I'll see you later." He kissed her again and then asked her to escort him to the door.

"Merry Christmas all," he said.

"Merry Christmas, Santa," we sang back.

"Look out of the living room window," he added as he departed my house.

We all gathered in my living room and waited while Santa said a no doubt lengthy goodbye to Fenella via tonsil tennis.

Eventually, she walked through to join us.

And then a sleigh pulled by reindeers including a red-nosed one slid through the newly fallen snow outside my window, before taking off into the air and disappearing over the trees. Stan waved to us from the back of it. From the engine at the back of the sleigh sparkles suddenly appeared spelling out:

MERRY CHRISTMAS, DELA. ENJOY THE MAGIC OF CHRISTMAS.

And as we all stood together hugging and crying with the sheer emotion of the day, I knew it would be my favourite day of the year forever more.

EPILOGUE

Dela

Six months later

"You may as well just officially move in," I said to the warm body whose arms I was wrapped in. Despite saying we'd take things slowly, Nick had stayed here every night. The one night he had tried to sleep at home he'd walked in and thought his dad was having a heart attack, until he'd burst into Stan's bedroom and found out he was having Fenella.

Since then he'd stayed here.

"Oh okay, if you insist," he said, smushing me in closer. "I reckon Fen will move in with my dad soon now. It wouldn't surprise me if by next Christmas she was the new Mother Christmas."

"I hope so. They both deserve to be happy. They do so much for others. Now, you'll have to excuse me, but I have to go to work."

"Only if you give me the secret password," Nick said.

"Is it blow job?" I asked.

"Nope."

"Do I get a clue?"

"It's the answer to this question. One day in the future when I propose, will you say yes to marrying me and having all of my babies, and will you be prepared to one day be married to Santa?"

"No," I said, and I felt him freeze.

"What?"

"No, I won't say yes one day in the future. I'll say yes now. I don't need fancy proposals or blingy rings. I already know that I love you and one day I'll marry you and have your babies and be Mrs Christmas, Stanley Nicholas Anderson."

His mouth came down on mine in a passionate, love-affirming kiss. "I love you too."

"You're not letting me out of bed now are you?" I said between kisses.

"Nope," he confirmed. "You're going to be very late this morning."

Ginny

"Ginny, any chance you can give me a hand with the shop this morning?" Callie said as I walked through the door. I'd called in for a red velvet cupcake and a pink lemonade, but there was a queue forming and no sign of either Dela or Aria.

"Sure," I said. "I'll run the bookstore. Where is everyone?"

"Dela's no doubt in bed, and Aria is sick. She's been vomiting all morning apparently."

I froze. Vampires didn't vomit. In the back of my mind was Merrin's words from last year. Then a customer asked me a question and I pushed it all to the back of my mind.

Jason entered the store. I remembered him from being an onlooker when the great undead and unwashed had talked to me like crap. God knows what he was doing being a friend to that... *thing*. One day I would make Merrin suffer because I'd not forgotten that day when he'd talked to me with such disdain. How dare he act superior to me. Me! I was a Letwine vampire.

Jason's phone rang and as he listened his face grew more panicked and he shouted out, "Oh shit."

"What's the matter, Jason?" Callie asked, rushing to his side.

"Alistair at the yard has just called. A load of the junk Merrin has stored just collapsed and Merrin is buried under it all. He can't die from it as he's already dead, but Merrin is extremely claustrophobic. We have to rescue him as quickly as possible. I need Nick and his expertise. Maybe he can use his digger to help."

"There's no need," I said, stepping forward. "Tell me where this place is and I shall go there immediately. I can easily rescue him using my superior vampire strength."

"Er, if you're sure..." Jason said slowly.

"I'm beyond sure. It would be my pleasure to help him," I declared.

And as Jason reeled off his address and I got ready to whizz over there, I smirked. It would indeed be my pleasure when I removed the crap covering Merrin and he saw just who had rescued him.

He'd be appalled.

And that made my dead heart very happy indeed.

THE END

Can Ginny and Merrin find a way to be around each other in Gnarly?

Find out in Suck it Up. Out 24 April 2022.

Pre-order here: https://geni.us/suckitup

ABOUT ANDIE

Andie M. Long is author of the popular Supernatural Dating Agency series amongst many others.
She lives in Sheffield with her son and long-suffering partner.

When not being partner, mother, or writer, she can usually be found on Facebook or walking her whippet, Bella.

SOCIAL MEDIA LINKS

Andie's Reader Hangout on Facebook
www.facebook.com/groups/1462270007406687
(come chat books)

Andie's Newsletter

geni.us/andiemlongparanormal

(get a free ebook of DATING SUCKS, a
Supernatural Dating Agency prequel on sign-up)

ANDIE'S OTHER BOOKS

Supernatural Dating Agency

The Vampire wants a Wife

A Devil of a Date

Hate, Date, or Mate

Here for the Seer

Didn't Sea it Coming

Phwoar and Peace

Also on audio.

Collection of Books 1-6 available.

CUPID INC

(Supernatural Dating Agency Spin-off series)

Crazy, Stupid, Lazy, Cupid

Cupid and Psych

<u>Sucking Dead</u>

Suck My Life – also on audio
My Vampire Boyfriend Sucks
Sucking Hell
Suck it Up

<u>The Paranormals</u>

Hex Factor
Heavy Souls
We Wolf Rock You
Satyrday Night Fever

Collection of all 4 books available.